Hidden Lives

Anthology

When the Streetlights Went On

End of Life

Three Days of Darkness

Jerry Pociask

Copyright © 2017 Jerry Pociask

This book is a work of fiction. Names, characters, places, and incidents are either products of the author's imagination or used fictitiously. Any resemblance to actual events, locals, or persons, living or dead, is wholly coincidental.

No part of this publication can be reproduced or transmitted in any form or by any means, electronic or mechanical, recording, by information storage and retrieval or photocopied, without permission in writing.

Published by Southern Owl Publications, LLC

Dedication

Writing a dedication is more difficult than writing a story! So many to be grateful to…so much to be grateful for. Having vicariously thanked the many, I offer my love to my son Jason, his wife, Lindsay, my daughters, Jessica and Catherine, grandkids, Kylan, Keedan, Aila, and sister Chris. Your help and confidence will never be forgotten.

When the Streetlights Went On

By Jerry Pociask

"He looked around at the perfectly white world, felt the wet kisses of the snowflakes, pondered hidden meanings in the pale yellow streetlights that shone in a world so whitely asleep.

"Beautiful," he whispered." ~Kurt Vonnegut

Copyright © 2017 by Jerry Pociask

This book is a work of fiction. Names, characters, places, and incidents are either products of the author's imagination or used fictitiously. Any resemblance to actual events, locals, or persons, living or dead, is wholly coincidental.

No part of this publication can be reproduced or transmitted in any form or by any means, electronic or mechanical, recording, by information storage and retrieval or photocopied, without permission in writing.

FOREWORD

I once read where technology advanced so rapidly in the 1990s the analogy was to compare the Wright Brothers first flight at Kitty Hawk to the Apollo 11 landing on the surface of the moon. In fact I have also heard that Apollo 11 had less computer power than a USB memory chip of today and certainly less than any current vehicle manufactured here or abroad. Apollo 11 had the same power computing capability as a handheld calculator.

Back then, I was convinced two soup cans strung along a space of fifty feet was technology unprecedented!

"When the Streetlights Went On," is not about making disparaging comments about technological advances, nor is it a baby boomers intention to point fingers at today's new leaders with remarks of, "That's not how we used to do it," or to start a sentence with, "Well, in MY day..."

Instead these are the recollections of a man who was raised in Detroit. The same place where cars are built, stars are made, especially Motown and during WWII, half of the tanks and planes were constructed, mostly by women.

Perhaps it is a time where we as children not only learned values but decided our own. Values that our parents questioned and later our children laughed at. But they were OUR values. We lived by them and with them. We still do. Perhaps that is why change for each generation is difficult. It is how phrases like, "That's not how we used to do it," became born.

This is a compilation of my memories of a great city. A city where memories still exist and will never die. I offer this caveat, they are my memories. Any similarities or opposing viewpoints are your own. I have even changed the names to protect the innocent except for my own and a few family members.

I have had the great fortune to travel and visit many major cities within the United States. I've been honored to meet many who also grew up in large metropolitan areas like Detroit, Chicago, Los Angeles, and D.C. During those times of travel, I discovered through conversations, the Boomers and later today's Millennials were often raised on a very simple cultural premise which was to be home at night when the streetlights go on.

Throughout the country I found similar stories, i.e. similar family values and experiences. So similar I must assume this story is nothing new and could be written by many people, living in numerous places. Probably in many eras as well, stories about sandlot baseball games or playing with dolls; hide and seek until midnight while parents sat on porches or stoops chatting with the neighbors, or walks in groups to the corner stores for a cream-filled cake and a soda, or "pop" if you prefer. In some areas of the country we drank sodas, in others we called it a pop. But the one common denominator I found across the metropolitan U.S. was the one simple parental commandment of, "Just be home when the streetlights go on."

~#~

The City of Detroit has good bones. I mean its rich in culture and history even before the War of 1812. A powerhouse in industry well placed along the lakes and rivers of the Great Lakes where abundant natural resources could be shipped around the world from Detroit locations. Eventually the city would become the fourth largest in the United States, boasting commerce, culture and growth. It is a city filled with immigrants, a mixed bag of traditions and opinions. My own ancestors came from Poland, "the old country" as proud immigrants referred to their countries of origin. While these immigrants assimilated into the new country, they also maintained traditions and prejudices to influence certain ethnic parts of Detroit.

Detroit had its triumphs and its failures like any city does. They had their industry and financiers; their poor and homeless. They even had a notorious gang known as the Purple Gang. For most it didn't matter what went on behind the closed doors. During prohibition, many were more concerned about the whiskey barges that came across the Detroit River from Windsor,

Ontario. Newcomer's came to the land of milk and honey to find and build a new life, and build they did.

During WWII, the available automobile manufacturing facilities built tanks and jeeps. Airplanes were built by "Rosie the Riveter," at plants in Ypsilanti. The country flourished and the citizens of Detroit never hesitated to pitch in for the war effort.

The end of the war was not lost to history. The country needed to rebuild and Detroit was once again in perfect position to contribute.

Through the '50s subdivisions were established to house the growing needs of the populations. Detroit expanded well beyond its initial boundaries. As families pushed these boundaries further out, housing, schools, hospitals and businesses flourished. At such times of growth, it was difficult to fail. To grow up in the 1950s kids were insulated from the horrors of war. We were treated to new inventions like television, which exploded the entertainment industry. Except in extreme circumstances, we never knew hardships.

Kids went to church, played outside with little or no supervision. Families ate dinner together and neighbors actually talked. We existed in a world of simple creativity thinking; a set of Lincoln Logs, an Erector Set or a "talking doll" caused us to implement our playtime with friends.

That was then. Times change; events change people. In all of this change, Detroit found itself trying to survive.

Hopefully these words will prompt you to re-live past experiences, triggering them to bubble upwards and explode in the realms of your present and past imaginations. It is in those very memories we've created a history which become our guidelines to help evaluate our present. During my lifetime I've learned the difference between perspectives and perceptions. Perspective can be defined by our senses of sight, smell, touch, hear and taste. Perception is how we define the experiences of those senses individually. Would there then not be congruence in a discussion about a blue shirt if one (or both), participants to a debate were color blind, have a cold, partially deaf or having something as simple as frozen fingertips? Does this example not open the possibilities of misunderstandings that become exponential as participants to a discussion are added? In my opinion, everything is open to debate; nothing is sacred or etched in stone. Even another person's opinion becomes subject to our own perspectives defined by our perceptions. Thus, a simple idea, you ARE what others want you to be, based upon how they "see" and what you are willing to allow/accept as their opinions.

So now, join me or us on a journey of the past as we share the forgotten, with a willingness to celebrate traditions we learned to let go of; to no longer want, or perhaps have been lost to technology.

~#~

It was fourth and ten. The perfunctory "huddle" completed. Sticks, hands, leaves, even used bubble gum represented each player on my team. Anyone privy to each huddle would expect to hear assignments doled out like this.

"Bob! You run exactly ten steps and cut left." I moved the bubble gum across an imaginary scrimmage line what was perceived as ten steps and slid it across to the left so I could be assured Bob knew exactly what I was saying. "Jim," I continued my directions this time with a small twig, "you stand next to Mickey as he hikes the ball. All I want you to do is run out like two yards and turn around." I pivoted the small twig, Jim also nodded.

"Tom, the game is almost over, the streetlights are going to come on in a few minutes." Everyone knew that anything we were doing would be "called" not because of darkness, but rather because of lights. To every kid standing in that asphalt street, there was a strict standing order given by every parent as we ran out the door in the morning, "Be home when the streetlights come on!" And now dusk threatened the ignition of that corner light, we knew we had only one more chance to win this game.

"Tom" I continued, "you're the leaf. I want you on the left side and you run the opposite pattern of Bob. Ten steps out, and cut right. Only when you do I want you to put a block on whoever is covering Bob. That should open him for the pass." Tom shuffled his feet knowing how serious of a task he had.

Then there was always the one kid, the one who was picked last for any event. They were overweight, slow and clumsy or just never had any athletic ability. They were always the one who asked, "What about me, what do you want me to do?" The answer was always the same, "Joe. You go long!"

I pointed one last time at the configuration of debris that represented our secret plans, "Everyone know what to do?" A chorus of yeses broke out; I carefully smeared the street with a bare hand to not give the "other side" any glimpse of our carefully laid plan. "Ok...on three then. BREAK!"

Street football never had an audible. Except I knew I needed to kill time. When the corner lamppost lit, the game was over. I was using a stall technique I knew I had just invented. Later I would learn it was as common as a cream-filled chocolate cupcake.

"Hup ONE!" I paused hoping to get the defense to draw an off side, "Hup TWO! Hup Three!" The football was always hiked from the side. Then tossed quickly so the kid hiking the ball could protect me from the kid who wanted a piece of my ass.

Each kid ran off from the line of scrimmage. Even the kid who "hiked" the ball was eligible as a receiver. I dropped back with that old leather football and watched my carefully laid plans slowly crumble. "Bubble Gum" took a step and tried to cut inside. "Twig" was rushed by a blitz and knocked on his ass. "Leaf" saw the rush and forgot to run the pattern. Instead, "Leaf" made a feeble attempt to block some new kid that must have weighed six hundred pounds and was also knocked on his ass.

There I stood, pumping a dimpled old leather ball searching for an open player. "Son of a bitch!" I thought. The one kid I didn't assign a piece of debris to was running for his life and was fucking open! NOBODY ever paid attention to the last kid picked, and yet there he stood, alone and in the open. With one last check, it was clear I had no choice. I pumped the football one more time and the lights went on. Eerily, Joe stood in a circle of light, alone and in the clear. Reaching behind me to gather momentum I threw the football as hard as I could. Stepping into the pass I watched the ball arc and spiral over everyone's head. Two defensive men looking stupid were wondering why the hell I was throwing the ball away until they saw Joe standing under the street lamp all alone. They both made a feeble attempt to run back and defend against him. I'm not sure why. That pass was officially known as the "Hail Mary Pass." You know the one, throw the ball as hard and as far as you can and pray anyone on your team is close enough to catch it! I

SWEAR after I threw the ball I looked at Joe standing there and he had his hands in his pockets!

That ball was thrown up perfectly. I think Joe pulled his hands out of his pockets, or maybe he opened one of them because, for some miraculous reason (prayers do work sometimes), Joe actually caught that pass!

I doubt anyone was more surprised than Joe that he caught that ball. Kids like him live for days just like this. He had "gone long" so many times he never really believed he would be thrown a ball let alone catch it. I guess kids in the 50's had learned hope. For this one time, that hope paid off and Joe was the hero. Everyone to a man walked over and punched Joe in the arm and congratulated him. He smiled and hugged that ball taking each punch and trying not to wince in pain. Joe stood in that circle of light like a rock star after a concert.

After each kid had punched Joe in the arm they casually walked over to pick up their "stuff" and headed home. Just a few more minutes would have parents standing on porches, hands on hips leering, wanting to announce the first warning quietly and eyeing the streetlight. We knew it was time.

We never really cared about the lights going on. It marked a time of day like ending a game of "hide-n-seek". The "home" was our base or goal. A safe haven when once there, nobody or nothing could "tag" you. The person who was "IT" were our parents. When the lights went on it was the same as yelling, "Olly, Olly Oxen Free!" our free pass home. It was the one constant. Nobody ever made fun of you because you had to be home. It was a code of honor respected by all. It marked the passage of another day.

Tonight would be no different. Leaf, Twig, and Bubble Gum would all go home and brag about Joe's impossible catch. That day Joe would never again be picked last for any team. He had earned the respect of many and a place of honor in the street football hall of fame.

~#~

Growing up through the '50s and '60s was both boring and exciting all wrapped into twenty some years.

It was a time of simplicity. The advent of suburban life that would eventually cause families to separate and pursue different avenues; the shopping mall replaced neighborhood stores where everyone knew the owner and the owner knew everyone.

Back then corner butcher shops flourished; drug stores were pseudo doctors' offices where a pharmacist dispensed drugs and advice without the need for a visit to the doctor first. (Ironic that today the top pharmacy chains now offer "nurse practitioner" services to alleviate the cost of a doctor's visit). The apothecary had huge five-gallon jugs filled with swimming black leeches sitting on the counter. I loved looking at the leeches squiggling around that jar waiting for their opportunity to play Dracula from a newly released Bela Lugosi movie. Doctors used to bleed bruises, black eyes or any sort of hematoma requiring removal of the dead coagulated blood under ones skin. I suspect today many would consider this as some sort of voodoo practice. Corner beer and wine stores were also willing to sell cigarettes to a minor with a parental note. Why? First off, the owner knew who our parents were. And second, the next time they saw our parents they would casually mention they sold us smokes, thereby "tattling" on us if the note was a forgery. If you hadn't figured it out yet, life was spent on street corners. Daytime was convenient. Nighttime was never sinister but lent a silent mystery to anything outside the round glow of the lamps on the sidewalks.

It was a time when we feared our parents' wrath if we got into trouble more than we feared the cops. It was a time for me when I learned values in life. Where my teachers were more than just my parents; we had extended families who watched over us, protected us, who helped other family and neighbors when in need. My parents, our families and close by neighbors all knew and lived by the adage of, "I got your back."

Computers were a thing of wonder and not convenience; it is very difficult to manipulate thumbs across an IBM punch card to send a message to the kid next door. Nope, had to either open a window and yell out to them or get dressed and go knock on a door.

The '50s were a time of sock hops, rock-n-roll, and naiveté. Cars weighed thousands of pounds and were powered by engines larger than today's "smart cars." Those cars had none of the technology equivalents of even a "smart phone," and sucked gallons of gas just to start 'em up. Seat belts? Fugedda about it. Baby car seats? Nope. A front seat in a '55 Chevy would easily sit 4 across and the back seat an army. (Which by the way was a real advantage at the drive-in movies).

The '60s brought in a new era starting with a Catholic President. Oh the horror of it all to think a president could be a Catholic. Makes me wonder what the reaction would have been if Martin Luther King Jr. ran for president and beat Obama as being the first black President. Unfortunately, we would never know just how good a president Kennedy would have been. His assassination shocked a world. The ensuing investigations, the alleged cover ups, the conjecture over his death, slowly began to split families and cities. The era of youthful exuberance and naiveté was crumbling. By the end of the '60s we all needed something to believe in, something to rally around and trust each other once again; in July of 1969 not only a nation but a world watch as Neil Armstrong stepped off the lunar lander and announced, "That's one step for man, one giant leap for mankind."

Today, even those words are in contention. Conspiracy theories about the moon landing abound saying the landing never occurred; it was staged as a movie set and NOT on the moon. Even now it is difficult to think the lunar landing occurred at some studio lot and was filmed as a hoax. Yep, naiveté died like the loss of virginity, i.e., once you lose your virginity you can never get it back.

~#~

The year I was born, 1953 was pretty much a dull quiet year for historic events. The world's population was at almost 2.7 billion, Joseph Stalin died and Dwight "Ike" Eisenhower was inaugurated, President. Richard Nixon was the Vice President and would make his own history some 20 or so years later. The Top Hit Song was, "The Song from Moulin Rouge," by Percy Faith and his

Orchestra. Later a remake performed by Christina Aguilera, Pink and a host of others was converted into a contemporary version showing some "skin." Back then the only hot bods we saw were actors like James Dean, in a sports cars and leather jackets. Marilyn Monroe standing over a subway grate having her dress lifted by the passing subway trains or from black market porn flicks imported from Mexico and Norway. Bill Haley & His Comets commandeered the charts as the rock-n-roll group and McDonald's would open their first stand in August of that year.

    Indeed, it was a dull quiet year. Many of the post war years were. People were still reeling from the attack on Pearl Harbor. After all that excitement and the ensuing war, slow and boring was the choice of many. Wounded men and women were slowly beginning to heal. As the economy grew so did the rest of the country. Turns out the economy was a great contrivance. Highways were funded and built allowing for greater cross country mobility. Families purchased new homes, automobiles and even splurged on a special vacation once in a while. As a kid? We never seemed to worry about anything, except the choice between a Twinkie cream cake, and a cream-filled chocolate cupcake. Perhaps we *were* naïve back then. Perhaps we still are.

~#~

I've invoked "artistic license" to create the nickname of "Tweeners." Tweeners describes the kids born in the early to late '50s. Meaning, they weren't at the leading edge of the Baby Boomers or the trailing edge. (By definition, a Tweener is a baby boomer born between the years of 1950 and 1958; i.e. born too late to be part of the "economic gravy train" and too early to become a part of the future tech explosion which today rules the world). The leading edge had the advantages of blossoming careers and opportunities. To "get a good job, get a good education" was the mantra for the much-needed teachers and nurses recruited from high schools and encouraged to make careers teaching or caring for the population growth. The only caveat here was the many men and women drafted or enlisted to serve in Viet Nam. Many kids from the poor areas of cities or from the fields and farms were drafted to fight a war that was the first to be shown on nightly TV.

The trailing edge of us saw the advent of twenty-four-hour news now being shown on sophisticated and expanding televisions. We were no longer relegated to movie house-news reels. The Boomers witnessed man landing on the moon plus the beginnings of a technological age that the "Tweeners" seemed to be skipped over.

Later in life, I would see my career stalled by men and women who were a few years older than I was, unwilling to step down or get out of my way. Today? According to the recruiters, I lack the technical training to compete with kids born even as early as the 1960s.

Perhaps "Streetlights" is my personal attempt at gaining back my own virginity, an attempt to simply assuage my own fears and bring back those memories and values that mattered to me.

Hopefully, as I stroll through the memories, the recollections of the events I will share, the reader will once again share and relive their memories. With any luck, this will elicit thoughts and stories we would all love to reminisce over. Computers make so much possible today I wonder if people would share their thoughts if they had to respond with a hand written, snail-mailed letter.

Regardless, I optimistically wish for you the reader to reminiscence some of the ideals of our own childhood. For those readers that are born in the '70s or later, perhaps this will be less of a history lesson and more an example of how you got to be where you are today.

~#~

July 20, 1969. I was anxious to get home and hopefully see the first moon landing. I did make it home early enough from my first job as a "window man" for McDonald's to see Armstrong take his first step on the moon. The old DuMont black and white television screen displayed Armstrong's leap off the ladder however, the audio never allowed us to hear his exact words, (of which were in contention until finally, some newscaster asked Armstrong what he said).

Watching this incredible event reminded me of the man who announced at the beginning of the decade that America would be the first to land on the moon. What ensued was an unprecedented space race with the U.S.S.R. and I was witness to that very success. I also remembered when the principal, Sister something or another from St. Suzanne's interrupted class to announce President Kennedy had been shot and we were all to start walking across to the church to pray. Yes, the churches always seemed attached to the schools back then. The priest was already leading a rosary to a church filled with nuns, teachers and students, some in tears and most in a state of shock. Maybe that was the day our virginity was stolen.

Nineteen Hundred and Fifty-Three may have been an uneventful year, but the years that followed slowly embellished and burnished memories which destroyed our naiveté even more. Maybe our innocence as well.

~#~

School reunions have an innate ability to cause one to reflect on their life. At the perfunctory "time for a shot of whiskey" all bellied up to the bar, a circle of friends gathered to reminisce. One story led to another. We laughed. We cried. We laughed again and then complained how our children have missed some of the finest things in life. We were disheartened that videos replaced backyards. Sandlot baseball had to become an organized sport. Kids no longer had to solve the problem of a torn cover on a baseball using stolen electrical tape from their dad's toolbox. That tape was the best and often times the only remedy to having a baseball to use in those days until they invented duct tape of course!

Certainly, uniforms were a dream of the "Barney McCoskey League," home plates with umpires, groomed diamonds with crisscrossed outfields. This was sandlot baseball; a game where anyone and everyone was Babe Ruth or Joe DiMaggio. Ironically we all wanted to eat Babe Ruth candy bars and as for DiMaggio? Every prepubescent kid had similar wet dreams about Marilyn Monroe.

But when it was time to "get up" a baseball game, no worries. Word traveled faster than text messages. We could get the word out and in less than half an hour we could field two full teams. Sometimes one or two of our dad's would stop by and become the home plate or first base umpire. If not, you batted until you either hit the ball or struck out. We played entire imaginary seasons, as well as a neighborhood World Series in an afternoon.

We had so much more freedom in the '50s and '60s. Without media driven paranoia, we never worried whose face was on milk cartons. We patrolled alleyways like green berets on a mission. Every house had a "rack" holding the old aluminum garbage cans in the alley. Did you know that an M-80 firecracker tossed inside an aluminum garbage can with the lid placed back; with a fat-ass like me sitting atop, an M-80 will blow the bottom out of said garbage can? Rumor was an M-80 was like a sixth stick of dynamite. Hey, it was never my idea.

The alleys were our way of moving from one house to another without the time wasting trips around a block. They were the "wartime tunnels" we hear about so much today. Wide open and very few secrets; well wait, there *WAS* that one secret about Mister and Miss <Cough>. Okay moving on here.

Hell, even our dads shared beers and shots of cheap whiskey with the neighbors across the alley. Mom's borrowed foodstuffs or soap from women they actually knew. Open the back gates and walk straight to a back door. Half the time no one knocked, just yelled out. "Anybody home?" instead of sending a warning via text we were a few miles away.

Yep, in the '50s and '60s people actually had real friends; not acquaintances. Neighbors weren't cut off from others by either expansive manicured lawns which replaced the old baseball diamonds to accommodate growth or electronic garage door openers which allowed a method of coming and going without ever seeing the people next door.

"History is supposed to provide knowledge of the longer context within which our lives take place. History is not just the evolution of technology; it is the

evolution of thought. By understanding the reality of the people who came before us, we can see why we look at the world the way we do, and what our contribution is toward further progress."
~ James Redfield, "The Celestine Prophecy"

~#~

The evening of my twentieth high school reunion, I realized how things had really changed. Stories of the past were replaced by job success, which included income and communal stature. Whether real or imagined, everyone believed the bullshit.

The nine hundred square foot bungalows were rapidly replaced by the twenty-four hundred square foot two story with its twelve hundred square foot attached garage. That evening was an evening of one ups-man-ship. It seemed we all fought for time to share our own special anecdotes, each becoming more and more embellished than the previous. Hell, we even had a television star attend the twentieth reunion.

Later, tired of hearing one more "yeah but" story, I raised a glass to toast the past. In honor of "Twig," Joe, "Bubble Gum" and the rest of us who had memories of times gone by, we raised our glasses. Some looked at me quizzically; others knew and understood the reason of the toast. It was really a toast to all of our parents alive and deceased. We missed those days of familiarity. The days when we knew we were safe and we had few rules. When we all agreed on the one universal rule, the rule that assured great torture and punishment meted out by everyone's parents equally if broken. That one rule was to be home as soon as the streets lights went on.

The mercury vapor lights on every corner and dispersed in the middle of the block were timed to go on at dusk; that was our curfew, our time to be walking through the door. "Come home when they flickered," every parent would order, "that way you are home when they are fully lit."

Standing at the bar rail six of us grown men shuddered at the thought of our dads greeting us at the door. If we were a minute past that first flicker there would be hell to pay. We never realized it back then, but that was the only way our parents knew we were okay. There were no cell phones. Unanimously we all agreed there was great security in that demand to be home.

Now a second round had to be ordered to celebrate reasons that were becoming less obvious. Alcohol has a way of clouding one's memory. For example, a simple walk in the park with a girlfriend can become a lifesaving event where each guy is the hero, his young lady the fair maiden. As all fairy tales follow, the maiden needs to find herself in danger for her knight to save her. Like most under the influence of alcohol, story lines blur and cross, opening an opportunity to introduce the story's villains. Myself I always hated the flying monkeys. Just seemed more appropriate saving a woman from lions and tigers and bears. That was kind of how the old high school stories rolled out. The kid who kicked a twenty yard field goal said it was a fifty yarder. A twelve second hundred yard dash was now in eight. And of course there were the usual stories about the dates that never really happened except in the minds of each one narrating. After a few more rounds we all started looking sideways at each other. Maybe it was easiest for us to focus on our conversations that way?

I just had a thought, those times growing up meant freedom. We were free to choose what we wanted. We made our own rules; we were creative. We were allowed to use our own imaginative devices to make a life. But the streetlights, the streetlights became a cardinal rule for our safety and our parent's peace of mind. They also marked a passage of time. Summers had longer days, therefore, we stayed out longer to play. Winter meant shorter days. The lights went on earlier because we still had school homework to do before going to bed. Maybe those seasons represented the passage to adulthood and responsibility? The lights were the one and only way we could be directed; a reminder of what to do, or suffer the consequences?

~#~

"The past is dead. Let the dead bury the dead." Og Mandino, "The God Memorandum, in The Greatest Miracle in the World"

It now occurs to me today's renaissance of Detroit is being created by the new wave of populations that in forty years will probably reminisce or lament about times past, much like I am doing today. My past and the events of Detroit's past are dead, time to bury the dead.

Ethnic Festivals are being replaced by electronic "movements." Old Neighborhoods are replaced with the newly renovated lofts; citizens are trendy, hip and younger. At one time I thought I was as well. The neighborhood bars, honky tonks, and strip clubs give way to "fusion" and finger sandwiches; all are well staffed and full of patrons. I still can't get past ear piercings the size of tire rims, nose piercings that remind me of a bulls ring but hell, my dad hated hair to my shoulders and my ruby red patent leather platform shoes. Briggs Stadium became Tiger Stadium; now Comerica Park with all the newness, attracts all the newest fans. It is time to pass the baton and appreciate the ideas and excitement of the newest generation of Detroit city dwellers. I laugh at myself because as the city changes and grows I find myself being negative about the change. It has NOTHING to do with the growth and everything to do with the change. Nobody likes to be reminded time has passed and we can't always do the same shit we have in the past.

Allow me instead to applaud the efforts of the Ilitch's, Penskes, and Gilberts. Welcome Shinola Watches and bikes. The shawarma and fusion, microbrews and distilleries. Add in the new parks, transportation hubs and entertainment venues, allow me to raise a glass in toast to Detroit's changes and success.

~#~

Discussing the '50s and the '60s to anyone having had the experience of them will usually elicit starry-eyed reactions. Some mixed with memorable disdain. "Oh man! I remember when..." is usually how a conversations begins then followed by strings of anecdotes which would fill pages of memories; prompting anyone else listening to add their own story. It became a game of "one upsmanship," as they moved from one story to the next. Or maybe we simply created those iconic "lightbulb" moments when our own lights when on?

In the '50s kids sat with a bowl of crisp flakes watching test patterns on black and white televisions until programming started at eight in the morning. It was always a bet as to when some distant television station would decide the start of their broadcast. There were no regularly scheduled programs, except for the nightly news. On weekend nights, we begged to stay up until midnight to hear the Star Spangled Banner play and watch fighter jets do "fly bys" over Arlington Cemetery. It was a sense of safety and comfort knowing those jets were flying over our heads. To this day, I never remember hearing one overhead, but it never mattered. We knew we were safe. I sometimes think we spent the entire day running and playing; sleep would overcome any outside interference or fears. I wonder if the word "insomnia" was a word in the dictionary then. Not sure if ADHD was a legitimate diagnosis yet.

One of the biggest concerns in the sixties was the threat of nuclear attack. Elementary schools had water and food provisions stashed in basement tunnels. They were designated shelters for everything from tornadoes to nuclear holocaust. I tried my damned hardest to convince my dad to build a fallout shelter in our basement or backyard. I was sure it was a great idea, not because I was afraid of the possible destruction of the planet, I saw a shelter as a place of my own where I could be alone, play my drums without complaint and just chill. In the event of a tornado or nuclear war, I guess I would have allowed the rest of the family inside; must have been a teenager thing happening back then.

~#~

When streetlights were in vogue, it was an easier time. Cars were made of pure steel and rubber. They weighed tons and not pounds. Their engines sucked high-octane petroleum faster than a starving baby from a mother's teat. We didn't worry about seat belt laws. We could head out to Woodward or Telegraph Roads and test the power of our 427 cubic-inch four barreled normally aspirated engines without fear or repercussion. The gendarmes left us alone. It was one of the rights of passage from boyhood to becoming a man. Cars became an extension of manhood (penis envy?), which fueled the growth of Detroit's ability to become the automotive capitol of the world. Imagine screeching tires down Telegraph or Woodward road in a pretend drag race after the lights turned green; never any winner or any loser. Traffic back then was "light" even though both roads were major feeders into the city or out of the state. Cruising the 'Graph or Woodward was this generations method of online dating. Every stop light represented an opportunity for a potential "hook up."

There was no difference of gender; male or female, it was a mobile party and we hung out windows screaming "I love you" to any car filled with the opposite sex. We all enjoyed a life of privilege. Frankly, back then, I remain unsure anyone really cared.

As with any generation, we all had our foibles and fables. A friend owned a yellow Fiat Spyder that took ninety degree turns at two thousand miles an hour! I swear it's true! It was a convertible. Yellow as a hornet and open aired. We cruised Telegraph in hard hats, drank beer, tossed empties over our head and into oncoming traffic; laughed our asses off the whole time. Once we stopped for gas at Seven Mile and Telegraph; not because we needed gas, but because I screamed "I love you" at two gorgeous blondes in one of their father's sedans. So picture this, they pull into a corner gas station and my buddy does a "YOOOWHEEE" in front of oncoming traffic so we can meet them under the pretense of needing petrol. As we circled the station and tried to start up the intro phase of the evening, we realized the two ladies were already "gassed". They over shot the pump island; the driver attempted to back up and align the car's tank with the pump. Problem was, she was too drunk to know better. She ran UP the island and knocked over the pump! Incredulous, my friend looked at me, I nodded and we sped off leaving the damsels in distress. Two miles later, I was screaming I love you to another carload of girls. Don't remember if we hooked up that night but we had fun.

Only once did I ever hook up. Well no, I didn't. A group of us guys went to Toledo, Ohio to some bar because they served 3.2% beer. On the way home, on Telegraph Road, by the way, two chicks cruised by us. I rolled the window down and screamed, "You like bikes?"

"Hell yeah!" was the reply. My friend's house was close. "Follow us!"

They did. My friend started his bike taking each for a ride. Only "hook up" I ever witnessed. Rumor was he ended up with a dose of clap later. Oh yeah, clap was curable with a stiff injection of penicillin and was never anything like the threat of HIV or any of that shit. Stay tuned; I'll talk about that shit in my next Streetlights of the '70s and '80s, hahaha hahaha.

Anyhow, on Telegraph Road, there existed a fable that every starry-eyed male teenager dreamed. To this day, I believe it was the story or fable the writers of "American Graffiti," stole from us Detroit boys.

Every Friday and Saturday night, we searched for that gorgeous blonde, driving a crisp Corvette with a sign attached to her plastic car that read, "IF you can beat me, YOU can eat me!" The first time I saw "American

Graffiti" with Suzanne Sommers in that classic T-bird scene, my boner lasted three days. I admit it OKAY!! Shit! I cruised Telegraph a couple of times after, for old time's sake and hoped, just maybe. I mean, "IF you can beat me you can eat me?" I would have been in more luck at Brush Street in Detroit and paying for it.

The "maybe" never happened.

Now, stop a moment. What eighteen to nineteen year old hasn't had wet dreams of such opportunities? Did we ever actually "see" her? Nope. But I can guarantee it became the legend of what made many "wet dreams".

I could go on and on about "Cruisin' the 'graph." Another great story was about how some dumb ass allegedly "flipped the bird" at a car filled with a bunch of guys. Evidently, one of the occupants mentioned, rather shouted out at the "flipper" his date was gorgeous. Anyway, after a normal circuit from Schoolcraft Road to Michigan Avenue, the car full of testosterone-driven young men saw the asshole sitting at the Palace Restaurant right by the window. His chick sat across from him; his trophy car all shiny and new was parked a mere few feet from their window.

As the story goes, one of the guys was a recent Viet Nam vet who made it apparent it was not a good idea to fuck with him. They passed the restaurant and recognized the convertible parked out front. The vet ordered the driver to turn around and go back. He instructed the driver to pull up next to the asshole's car. To the total disbelief of everyone watching the vet climbed atop the hood and proceeded to defecate on the windshield and hood. The dude in the restaurant pasted his face against the window screaming. His date was laughing her ass off. Adding insult to injury, the guy from Nam rips his t-shirt off, wipes his ass and tosses the shirt onto the driver's seat. GOD I wish I could have seen that!

"When you're young, you think everything you do is disposable. You move from now to now, crumpling time up in your hands, tossing it away. You're your own speeding car. You think you can get rid of things, and people too, then leave them behind as well. You don't yet know about the habit they have, of always coming back. Time in dreams is frozen. You can never get away from where you've been."

— <u>Margaret Atwood</u>, <u>*The Blind Assassin*</u>

Back then, sensory overload wasn't known. Computers and cell phones were inventions of the future. If you wanted to call a friend you walked to their house, stood out front and yelled their names, or parents stood on the porch calling us in the same way. Nobody rang bells or banged pots. You simply walked up to or over to the person you needed to speak to and knocked on the door or punched them in the arm.

Neighbors mowed their lawns because they respected the other neighbors. You would never think of leaving trash in a yard. People took pride in what they had.

One neighbor grew vegetables in his backyard instead of grass. Corn stood ten foot high while tomatoes and beans were ruby red and stalks that reached the giant's castle in the sky. This elderly gentleman was excused from having a well-manicured lawn. For that matter, nobody cared he even had a lawn. I mean, why have grass when he had his own "farmers market" on Grandville? My mom would send me over with two quarters and I'd come back with a twenty-pound paper sack filled with beans, peas, tomatoes, and corn. "Thank ya," was always the response, "Pays for me seeds."

Unemployment or Union strikes brought neighbor-aid with offerings of food, cash or odd jobs to help. One wasn't a pariah for not working. People didn't define themselves by what they did for work. They defined themselves by who they were; a mom, a dad, a sister or brother. Extended families mattered; they all lived close. Everyone could trust we would be the person we were yesterday, today and tomorrow. Well, almost.

"It is easy, when you are young, to believe that what you desire is no less than what you deserve, to assume that if you want something badly enough, it is your

God-given right to have it."

— Jon Krakauer, *Into the Wild*

~#~

Naive..."Webster" 2-deficient in worldly wisdom or informed judgment.

That is what we were, naïve. We had no need to be "in the know". It was sufficient to wait until your party line cleared to place a phone call. Party lines were shared phone services; the "sharer" was most likely the lady across the alley who your mom borrowed that cup of powdered soap from. When they terminated their call, you had a clear avenue to talk to anyone you wanted. Can you imagine that today?

The only irritating part of having a "party line" was the constant picking up of the phone and checking to see if anyone was still using the phone line. It could be fun, you could listen in on conversations; until either you or them, bluntly announced, "I am on the line!" Some people made it a game to see how quietly they could lift the old receiver and see if they could listen in on your call. The dog barking in the background always gave them away however. I guess it was the equivalent of modern day text snooping. Ah, the exquisite and delicious aspects of the neighborhood gossip.

The irony was we didn't have a need to connect to the world back then. Walter Cronkite or the Chet Huntley/David Brinkley Hour was sufficient in showing us the world's negatives. So why would we want more? I do remember Cronkite announcing the assassination of President Kennedy and being duly saddened by the tears Cronkite shed. Later he would go on to keep the world informed about Viet Nam.

~#~

During my stint at St. Suzanne's my only worry was whether or not I could execute the infamous "shuffle step" for the St. Suzanne's dance recital. Viet Nam was a long way away for me and Kennedy had already been laid to rest in Arlington where we watched the jets fly over every Friday and Saturday night.

There is a point I want to inject here. Friday and/or Saturday pizza was an incredible treat back then.

IF you wanted a pizza delivered by say eleven PM, you called in the order around five or six that evening and sat waiting in anticipation; hoping you didn't fall asleep before it arrived. Thus the success of Tom Monaghan and Domino's Pizza ™ who declared delivery in thirty minutes or less or it was free. Since he started in Ann Arbor and Ypsilanti with a college populace, he became an instant success.

Oh yeah, the "shuffle step", the recitals had nothing to do with being laughed at or ridiculed for doing a two-step or a tap. We had our own enemy watching over us; I feared Sister Anna Marie would wallop the shit out of me with her four-foot oak poker for stepping when I was supposed to be shuffling.

Naive were my parents as well. They paid good money for my parochial education back then. I think they actually believed I was getting a better foundation, a better education than the "they" of the public system. I now see that my mom and dad believed having my hands slapped with a ruler 23 kabillion times was actually good for me. I don't know, perhaps they thought Dominican nuns could actually be surrogate parents. Dominican nuns sucked at being parents. Maybe that is why they became nuns?

Naive was thinking that nuns, who wore habits covering every inch of their body in black and white except hands and a small moon of a face, actually had legs let alone breasts.

To a first or second grader, they floated along the ground like a specter. To a seasoned seventh or eighth grader, their cover was blown.

I will never forget the first time a nun adjusted her Alb and I saw her boobs frocked under another hundred layers of cloth. I mean like holy shit! They actually were real women under all that cloth! And to think, we all thought they were hired as constables with the power to castrate even the manliest of men with a quick slash of that four-foot poker. But there they were...BOOBS! I'll be damned, boobs. Sure as hell those boobs didn't give me the same reaction as when Maria, Susan or Nancy walked past my desk. But, none the less, those were real boobs!

Speaking of Mary, Susan or Nancy? Like every immature young man I was SURE those boobs were real. Hell! Who knew then that thirteen-year-old girls were already stuffing themselves to try to look attractive to our young male egos? During the afternoon's Math class when Mary helped pass out mimeographed test copies that smelled like ethanol, who noticed they never bounced? My mind was somewhere off in some exotic place thinking Mary "wanted" only me and me ONLY! Ohhhh to see 'em for real. Oh god was I inexperienced! I was no different than any other prepubescent asshole.

~#~

Wait a minute. I was just slapped across the face. All of the neurosis that exists in this world is NOT from some form of abuse. It's NOT from being hit more than once with a four-foot poker. It's from spending our test days sniffing the chemicals and inks of all the old mimeographed sheets of paper! It's no wonder a number of those raised in the '50s and '60s joined the drug counter culture. They were hooked in the elementary school systems mimeograph machines producing handout sheets. That would also explain why the "teacher's pet" was the "teacher's pet!" They didn't just want to kiss ass and wipe blackboards. NOOOOO! They wanted to be locked in the mimeograph rooms and spend eternity in mimeograph heaven!

~#~

I may have mentioned before "When the Streetlights Went On" is a compilation of memories. Mine of course and subject to my own prejudices based upon my own perceptions and perspectives. Nothing here is meant to be inspirational. It's a compilation of memories in those sandlots. The memory of being fourteen and driving my father's car to the corner to present a written note to the storekeeper, giving me permission to buy my mom cigarettes. There are memories for the young ladies of being fitted for their first bra, or better yet from my perspective, the first time I actually touched that first breast. Many memories we may only be able to share secretly because the event was so solemn one wouldn't dare speak of it aloud. "When the Streetlights Went On" hopefully will allow the children of the '50s and '60s, see how their lives made a mark on society and its culture; restore their faith in the human spirit.

> "Everything's just fucking *Disney* with you."
> Nenia Campbell, *Horrorscape*

Yeah, it is!

~#~

> "The main reason Santa is so jolly is because he knows where all the bad girls live."
> George Carlin

#

Ahhh, the Christmas Season, my favorite time of year! Starting with Thanksgiving, and ending on January 6th, our holiday seasons were likened to a dance marathons, but only for food. I like this metaphor; it reduces my guilt for when I step on that scale every morning to weigh myself. Now I get to project all my guilt back onto my mother. Come to think of it, I can spread some of that guilt along with the yellow capsule colored margarine recommended by the FDA and my grandmother who *forced* me to eat 87,000 apple pies.

Thanksgiving was the starter pistol whose shot rang "in" the beginning of the eating marathon. Relatives buried faces in twelve-inch plates, sucking up roasted turkey, city chickens, mashed potatoes slathered in butter and gravy, polish kielbasa a yard long and the perfunctory vegetable i.e., green beans soaked in Campbell's mushroom soup (WITH SODIUM of course); buried in battered and fried onions. I had an uncle who at age 30 weighed 975 pounds! Or maybe he really only weighed 450 pounds. But to a cherubic 3-year-old it, perspectives said 975. He was always the winner of the holiday feasts.

That uncle was a great guy, but damn he could "pound" the food. He used two eating utensils, a fork and a slice of pumpernickel bread held in his left hand. It was a makeshift ladle which, used in unison with a fork, allowed him to shovel food in faster and easier than my mom could produce in bowls set on the table. I remember sitting in utter amazement that any human could consume such vast quantities of mashed potatoes. I always wondered why my parents went to a farmer's market to buy produce for the winter. Years later I realized they were saving up for the holiday dinners.

"You are fettered," said Scrooge, trembling. "Tell me why?"
"I wear the chain I forged in life," replied the Ghost. "I made it link by link and yard by yard; I girded it on of my own free will, and of my own free will I wore it."
Charles Dickens, "A Christmas Carol"

In this uncle's defense, it wasn't link by link as exclaimed by Jacob Marley, (well maybe kielbasa links), and it was pound by pound.

~#~

Reminds me of the number of times my mom bought a bushel of pickles at Eastern Market in Detroit and then spent a Saturday cooking up brine to make her own dill pickles. We had like a twenty-gallon crock where these pickles would marinate, slowly absorbing the dill, garlic and vinegar brine. All I remember was the flavor was incredible and the freshness incomparable! *THE* best in the world of course. If you are thinking the house would be permeated with the wonderful aroma of pickles fermenting imagine the smells of twenty gallons of cabbage fermenting into sauerkraut.

Sometimes my mom and dad would buy heads of cabbage and sit straddled on a slaw shredder, rocking back and forth in a seesaw motion, dragging the cabbage head across very sharp blades. The shredded cabbage would build on a clean sheet below and be prepared for making sauerkraut.

Who gives a shit? Nobody today. Those pickles and sauerkraut were staples back then. We didn't always walk to the store to fill our needs. Hell, "Wonder Bread" was like eating cake. We had a cache of staples which represented security in the worst of times. Screw the stock market. Nobody cared. What mattered was being able to feed a family. And we had pickles and sauerkraut to permeate and punctuate our memories.

Then came Christmas Eve, my dad had two brothers who never married. Every year they would come over for a standing rib roast dinner. Uncle John and Uncle Stan were bachelors and I suspect had three decent meals a year. Many years later as I cleaned out the respective apartment of a deceased uncle, I found handwritten notes from Uncle Stan ordering three White Castle burgers with a large coffee whitened by triple cream; inconsequential I am sure, except I must have found over 100 hand written notes on scraps of paper and old White Castle napkins. Oh yeah, Uncle Stan left the army after the "big one" and moved into the Clark's Park YMCA in Detroit. A 12 by 10 room was his life for over 50 years. A bed, a dresser, one chair and a hot plate served as his personal belongings; a window ledge in the winter a refrigerator. There was no in room plumbing or private shower. Later, out of respect for my uncle, the "Y" saved his room as the last rental, while the rest of the rooms became transitional housing for felons and juvies.

As for Uncle John? He lived with my parents for a short time. Everyone said he was weird. I guess he was.

He once told my dad he was being followed by spies. War stories of being chased by two Germans for a few days probably supported today's diagnosis of post-traumatic stress so many men and women suffered in our wars. When he passed, his apartment was a mess. Aisles carved through his "stuff" allowed passage through his condo. A basement full of empty beer bottles…6 trips and hundreds of bottles later I added over $500 to his estate at one 10 cent bottle return at a time.

~#~

Christmas Eve was my time for the old "A Christmas Carol" movies on the old Dumont black and white TV. I watched it every year while getting ready for Christmas dinner at my grandmothers. Mom would dress early while preparing dinner for my uncles. A fifth of Crown Royal seduced a father and two brothers, once or twice with my mom to toast the holiday, only to be chased with either beer or Jim Beam, (Uncle Stan's favorite and to this day mine as well), highballs mixed with Canada Dry Ginger Ale. God, I loved that night.

The smell of a roast in the oven and the anticipation of grandma's apple pie made my salivary glands swell.

Dad would be busy filling highball glasses; topping off shot glasses thinking of ways to toast the holidays. My sister had her own room upstairs and she spent her time readying herself there. Oh yeah, it was years later I found out that was where Santa hid all the gifts. I never went up there so it was a perfect hiding place. Made me wonder what else was hidden in the old eaves.

Anyway, On Christmas Eve I sat blissfully watching the old reruns of Scrooge. I had seen it so many times I could quote the dialogue.

Later in the early evening, after dad and my uncles had shared a few good stiff drinks or shots with beer chaser's, it was time to head over to grandma's house for some serious food and partying. Looking back, I now wonder how we got there.

"T'was the night before Christmas and all through the house," those words are the beginning of perhaps one of the most memorable stories of all time.

And why not, the story is all about being a child again. For one time a year, it is okay to believe in Santa Claus. To relive past memories or to replace some memories we wished we never had. Regardless, the story was written for those of us who have become too busy, too stressed or simply too old to care.

Charles Dickens also wrote, "A Christmas Carol" as a reminder of what is truly important in life. In fact, IF I were a retailer, I would have the ending of that movie on a closed loop tape playing all over my store! The monolog ends the movie saying how Scrooge changed his way and became a great man in spite of his past. He became symbolic of joy, laughter, and giving! He realized *what* was important in life and shared not only of his money but of himself.

As a kid growing up in Detroit, our actual Christmas always started at about three in the afternoon Christmas Eve and ended after the second wave of food, spirits, and gifts at about eight o'clock at night Christmas day.

As previously mentioned, Christmas Eve always started with my two single uncles arriving around three to share some holiday spirit. To enjoy a standing rib roast with ALL the fixing's, some holiday time with a brother; all with a well-lit tree and annual decorations. Both being bachelors I doubt either one even hung a plastic candy cane on a door let alone decorate a tree. So I already knew this evening held special meaning.

My sister would ready herself in her upstairs lair and I used the spare room with the television on so I could dress watching Alastair Sims in the earlier version of Scrooge. Getting dressed had become a ritual. I had already removed the double-edged blade from my dad's razor, applied Barbasol Shaving cream and pretended to erase the imaginary "whiskers" that hadn't even yet become peach fuzz. I even recall secretly splashing some of my dad's Old Spice thinking nobody would know. Unlike the movie "Home Alone" there was no sting because at least I was smart enough to have removed the razor blade. I guess that movie employed "artistic license" to achieve cinematic results. I swore I smelled like a French whore and yet, nobody ever said a word.

By around six we all loaded up into a green '55 Chevy until I was almost ten; then a '59 Ford when I turned twelve. (New cars were out of the question. Dad refused to spend that kind of money when he knew he could fix and keep any car running like a top. Perhaps a future blog will be about his "prized '66 Chevy Caprice" that I manage to alter the bumper on one night).

Possibly Christmas was easier then. Less stress, fewer choices and families still lived within a five-mile radius. Sometimes we had to eat in shifts. I know I had to wait years until I was old enough to graduate to the adult table. Until then it was a two by ten spanning three or four wooden crates for our bench seat. It didn't matter; sisters, brothers, cousins, aunts, uncles, and friends were all gathered to enjoy the food, the drink and each other. And presiding over all of this was the family matriarch, a woman who single handedly raised seven of her own children and two foster kids. It just never got any better.

Along the way to grandmother's house it was a ritual to drive the "Tour de Oakman." Essentially the precursor to today's neighborhood Christmas lights competitions. Always a pre-requisite to the Christmas Eve festivities, the one-mile stretch was festooned with lights and decorations. Nothing had changed. Every neighbor attempted to outdo the others. After perhaps five years, or what seemed like twenty to a young man, the ultimate winner was always a corner sprawling ranch home. On top the roof was a Santa, his sleigh and his eight tiny reindeer. Nothing special as a lawn ornament but, this was on top the roof, well-lit and animated. Rudolph's nose even glowed.

The line of traffic usually moved along steadily until the Rudolph display. Every child begged their dad to slow or stop long enough to inhale the beauty and fantasy of a Santa atop a house roof with animated reindeer galloping into the night to help deliver presents. I also suspect each vehicle had a dad driving impatiently, rolling his eyes at having seen the same display one hundred thousand times in the past, or perhaps twice already this season. Yet, every car we passed had children's noses plastered on fogged windows gazing at each display. We all were amazed and anxious about the next day's anticipated presents. Much like most family rituals, the drive down Oakman Boulevard became a tradition never to be missed. Thankfully for my dad, this trip was along the way, not even a detour to grandma's house. He only had to endure the repeat of the annual ooh's and ahh's my sister and I mouthed at each new lawn and light display.

~#~

"Over the river and through the woods to grandmother's house we'll go, the horse knows the way," sorry no horse and no sleigh here.

My Grandmother lived in an old wooden framed house that was the first on the block to be built. My Uncle George spoke of how it started as a two bedroom and as the family grew the second half of the house grew. Evidently, it was also the first home built on the block that was initially a farm. So when the City of Detroit decided to plat map the street, they made a slight curve to accommodate my grandmother's house. All here say and conjecture at this point, but doesn't the romance add to my story? Also according to my uncle, there was a small pond in the back of the property that he swore was the reason why he loved fishing so much. All I can say is this, as Detroit grew, much of the land that MAY have at one time been a "dumping ground" was filled in. The pond is gone and replaced by wood framed and brick houses all in a row and in perfect alignment.

It would be years later when I was maybe eight, my mom or my aunts, or maybe a neighbor shared pictures of my mom and dad on the front porch on their wedding day. My dad was still in the Army and wearing his uniform. Mom wore the long veiled flowing wedding dress of the day. I still have pictures of her train that would cover about three acres of land. Then I was treated to picture after picture of every major life event from the '30s and '40s. Aunts, uncles, weddings. The difference was the same people aged over time. The one thing that never changed was Christmas dinner at Busia's, (Grandma's).

Dinners were always the same, the menu, the hard-planked seats, the gingham oilcloth that covered the table, the stove and ovens both in the kitchen and the downstairs basement were churning out heat enough to turn off the central heat even in the coldest of winters. Familiarity did hold some comfort for all of us. As I recall. The food became a process, a celebration of time. Opwatki, a blessed thin wafer, was broken off and shared along with a Christmas greeting by all. Then, black mushroom soup made from illegally imported mushrooms lovingly sent from overseas relatives. Screw Cuban cigars; give me the mushrooms. Kielbasa was made by Uncle Louie who owned a small butcher shop on Stahelin in Detroit. He packed his sausages in the store and then smoked them in his own yard all year long. Imagine what the neighbors, the EPA and perhaps even the FDA would have to say about that today.

But after the soup, the tender slow cooked ham was served with mountains of mashed potatoes. A roaster full of galobki's, ceramic dishes filled with cheese, potato and sauerkraut pierogi's, all boiled and fried in pure butter and sweet onions. Pickled herring in sour cream, pickled salads, cole slaw, buckets of gravies, Polish rye breads and imported butter. Laughter, stories and beer were passed around the table until it was time to serve the usual comfort foods. Pies, cakes, fried twisted dough sticks known as "angel wings," were plated and pushed down already full bellies. Certainly NOT heart healthy, gluten free, fat free, or anything free. Just damned good eating.

All these foods filled the air with superb aromas. As the smells wafted through the house, we swore it made the neighbor four doors down salivate. (BTW…within an hour that or many a neighbor would be over and join in the festivities). Basement feasts were always able to add another sawhorse and a two by ten seat. This was never a 12-minute football half-time meal. It was a process that took sometimes over two hours. Childhood stories of oranges and apples given as gifts during the depression were never interrupted even to ask to have the gravy passed. We sat in awe at how our parents ever made it through that time. And never once was there a complaint. And then we were treated to the personal stories told by neighbors who reminisced of their lives and the times shared with the very people at that table

It was obvious there were great feelings of love. I grew up happy and content, perhaps even immature thinking everybody shared a Christmas like this. The examples set forth by two generations made a lasting impression on all of the children which to this day are carried forth with our own families.

So you see, when I hear the beginning of the poem, "T'was the night before Christmas..." it brings me back to what I think many of us yearn for. Those simple times and memories...the sense of magic that existed when we believed there WAS a Santa Claus! The magic for some which may have been lost and yet to be found. For those of you longing to know more? Call me...I'll send you "T'was the Night Before Christmas" and if you don't believe, remember the "ghost of Christmas future" is a friend of mine.

Hold on. I forgot one last tradition. In 1934 the Ford Motor Company re-construction of a "rotunda." Resembling the number of automobile gears they manufactured and used in their vehicles, that structure was reconstructed in the Detroit area and became known as the Ford Rotunda.

Before Cobo Hall became infamous for the International Auto Show, the "rotunda" hosted the new releases of automobiles, and other press related needs.

For me it was a part of Christmas. For the rest of America it became the fifth most visited site in America surpassing Mount Vernon, Yellowstone, the Statue of Liberty and even the Washington Monument. Constructed in 1932 for the 1934 World's Fair in Chicago it was dismantled and reassembled in the Dearborn, Michigan area near Greenfield Village and the Henry Ford Museum.

Driving past the Rotunda at night was magical all year long. The upper three tiers were lit in changing colors making it appear as a giant birthday cake. It wasn't until years later I discovered, Albert Kahn, the architect, designed the outer shell to look like a mechanical gear. I cared less about cars even then. It was Christmas that drew me there. A forty-foot tree in the middle and the wonder of what would be new in the displays every coming year. With my sister, we stood mesmerized, in awe at the technical innovations that eventually would lead the world into mechanical and technologic change.

Every season children and adults alike stood in front of a forty foot decorated tree. The tree skirt was a layer of fake snow hiding the runners and tracks of animated figurines spinning and twirling on spindles that were probably "programmed" by early computers; if not the die makers of Ford Motor spent hours cutting schematics for the actions figures to follow. It didn't matter. I was mesmerized. It doesn't matter today. Back then I was content.

We all laughed watching as the "skaters" had worked their way around piles of wrapped gifts under the tree. I don't know about the other kids, but I remember thinking and wishing even just one of those gifts were mine. Not because they contained any major surprise, but because they were meticulously wrapped in papers and ribbons that would enchant any child of any age at any time!

In November of 1962, millions of visitors were captivated by the Ford Rotunda. Unfortunately, before Walt Disney could become a household name the Rotunda burned to the ground, never to be resurrected. That fire destroyed a part of many children's memories having a belief in Santa Claus. Nobody ever thought such a calamity possible.

~#~

Christmas was never Christmas without a visit to Hudson's Department Stores in the great city of Detroit. Mom, Chris and I took a bus to admire all the decorations that rivaled FAO Schwartz of New York. This was an excursion rather than a run to the mall sort of event. A forty-five-minute bus ride with at least one transfer, culminating with lighting a candle at St. Aloysius church then followed by a donut at one of the old donut shops on Washington Boulevard. It was the ONE time my mom allowed me caffeine. I mean it was a donut that needed to be dunked! Yet I lied, it wasn't the only time I was allowed caffeine. My Uncle Stan spent time in the UK while in the Air force and he taught me how to drink sweetened tea with cream. So when he visited, he always made me a cup along with his. When he visited I felt like I was Chinese visiting the opium dens. I loved the tea he made and to this day still, drink it the same!

If the '50s and '60s weren't magical, they were memorable. Tradition defined events. We actually sat down on Sundays for dinner. My mom, (June Clever), my dad, (Ward) and my sister well umm, err ah Eddie Haskell? I was the "Beaver." Take your pick of shows; they all fit the families of the times, "Ozzie and Harriet", "Donna Reed". It was a time when the rules were defined. Streetlights went on? Go home. Catholic school? A shirt and tie. Holidays at Busia's? Every darn cousin, aunt and uncle there to share; regardless of past hurts or angers, they were always healed, buried or dealt with at the holidays. There was no bullshit. There were arguments of course, but there was never a pretense.

Everything was tossed on the table to be examined, talked about, cried over and finally understood, forgiven. Then we moved on. That in my opinion, is survival. The continuity of families.

Today there are fewer families. Jobs take us not only to other cities or states but now even countries. Yes, we have the ability to be transported via airplanes, but a six to fifteen-hour commute for a weekend visit remains. Versus a fifteen-minute drive across town. The technology back then was never an option, yet today, I see how the Ford Rotunda, Disneyworld, computers, and even telephones became a divisive device. Fantasies lead to dreams, which lead to goals, which lead to change.

Merry Christmas, Wesołych Świąt, Happy Holidays, Felice Navidad, It mattered not how it was said. I said it as my sincerest wish for peace and happiness for everyone.

~#~

I suppose I should clarify the name grandma or grandmother. For anyone born second generation Polish, we didn't call grandma, Grandma. In Polish she was

Busia. Grandfather was Dziadzia. I'll save the next chapter for the paternal side. So there we were, all dressed in our Sunday best, dad half shit faced from toasting his brothers and mom proud as shit for serving them the one and only best meal of the year. Sis dressed in whatever sisters wore back in the fifties and I, sitting in the back of an emerald green '55 Chevy Bel Air locked and loaded for all the Faygo "red pop," plus anything else Busia threw down on the table.

    Christmas Eve was an eclectic mess of people on my mom's side. In today's "McMansions" I wonder how we ever catered to 25 people in less than 600 square feet. The answer was obvious...saw horses, 2 x 10's and crisp tablecloths, card table chairs, chromed vinyl covered chairs and even a few cinder blocks holding spare 2 x 10's sufficed. Norman Rockwell would have given his left arm for a picture of Busia's Christmas Eve table. Plates of ham and turkey, pierogi's, bowls of gravy, stuffed cabbages, mashed potatoes and kapusta dripped on those gingham oilcloths and no one gave a shit. It was CHRISTMAS!

After dinner and when everyone was fully satiated, my aunt would always break out the old Christmas Carol songbooks. Some of us would sit by the tree singing Silent Night, Deck the Halls or Silver Bells, while my mom's brothers and my dad sat around sharing more highballs.

One of the best parts of that evening was being able to stay awake and attend the St. Stephens midnight Christmas mass in POLISH. The lights. The Polish Christmas carols, the aroma of cheap Kessler's whiskey on the breaths of teetering old men. Ah, such memories for an eight-year-old kid who lived on the fringes of Detroit, that may as well have been in the boonies, enjoying his visits to the inner city.

Even then, when it snowed the city was quiet. Streetlights were lit but never overwhelmed the beauty of trees and outdoor lights lit all night on Christmas Eve through Christmas Day. My grandmother lived about two blocks from St. Stephens. The walk was easy enough and a welcomed reprieve for a young lad who just spent six hours in a hot, smoke-filled house with thirty odd others. It was a beautiful thing.

The church is still there today red brick with spires holding crucifixes atop the cupola-like roofs. A convent housed nuns who were there as teachers, neighborhood ambassadors, and disciplinarians. The rectory, of course, was for the "assigned" parish priests and the visiting priests who were there on assignment, internship or vacation. At that time they all spoke English and Polish, which didn't matter in a predominantly Polish neighborhood. In later year Spanish was introduced. The ethnicity changed.

Today when I drive past, the memories take me back. I marvel how my mother who was born in 1920 could have been baptized, confirmed, married and buried all at that one church. I was convinced if they had their own cemetery, she would have insisted she be interred there as well, but once again times change.

I attended St. Suzanne's elementary school. Founded in 1946 by predominantly Irish Catholics, the ethnic shift changed the ambiance of the old inner-city parishes. Living on the outskirts of the Detroit proper, for all intents and purpose we may have well been a suburb. Gone were the familiar duplexes. The wooden homes were all being replaced by the modern 950 square foot brick bungalow. Churches and schools sprouted like weeds in every neighborhood. St. Suzanne's became a part of the scenery. For me it was a great place to play in the schools parking lot. Much beyond that my basic memories included learning to pull my hands back from the wooden ruler that was about to discipline my fingers, the "fall-out shelter signs in the basement and the tissue stuffed bras I admired yet never did get to confirm.

Thinking of one of the shelters, I always wondered how long water would last or what sort of food could sit in 35-gallon cardboard drums for years and still remain potable or edible. At least we knew in the event of a nuclear attack the kids were safe. Never mind the psychological impact of three hundred kids worried and crying in wonderment about the rest of their family. It didn't matter though; we figured the Dominican nuns would keep order with their stern looks and raps on knuckles with wooden rulers.

~#~

My extended family was unusual; two uncles and two aunts who never married. One uncle who was married and no children. Three brothers, an aunt and my mom added 23 kabillion cousins to the mix. For a kid growing up in Detroit in the 1950s my family was like winning a lottery. Uncle Stan bought one of the first Mustangs produced. Uncle John took me to a game preserve to hunt. Uncle George and Aunt Agnes were my surrogate parents. Aunt Agnes my Godmother, Uncle Stan my Godfather and Uncle George was my sponsor for confirmation into the Catholic Church. All the first cousins were not only family but friends. Brother-in-law's and sister-in-law's were never prejudicial toward anyone in the family. Outside the family? A different question. But inside the family, was "tight." We all did things together which bonded family members and at times became quite educational.

For example, Uncle Stan loved thoroughbred horseracing. He often took me to Detroit Race Course or Hazel Park to watch the ponies run. An uncle and nephew bonding around animals; of course there was the math education, learning how to calculate odds and pay off at say four and a half to one with a fifteen dollar bet. Oh, the stares we incurred back then. Yet neither he, myself nor my parents gave this excursion another thought.

I actually did learn math and critical thinking by calculating odds and studying the field of riders and their horses from information gleaned about the jockeys and horses about their previous rides found obtained in the "programs". For example, the success of a horse's run in excellent conditions versus rainy or muddy conditions would cause an addition or a reduction in a handicap at the betting office. So did the experience of each jockey. By extrapolating the jockey's riding prowess and experience, plus the willingness of a horse to run in certain conditions, we could interpret the odds of success. (I should offer another caveat here, Uncle Stan never allowed me to bet. He always bet, however, he would ask me questions based on previous performances of the jockey's, the horses, track conditions and all the other factors). I got pretty good at it too. One time Uncle Stan asked me about a particular horse and if I would bet his "nose." After careful and diligent study, thinking I had just been entrusted to decide the fate of the world, ummm, Detroit, well maybe the race track, I solemnly stated I would place a bet on that particular horses "nose" for two whole dollars!

The odds were fairly a long shot at twelve to one. But the horse had been performing well with this jockey and had over 5 wins in its last eight starts. So confidently I told my uncle to bet two bucks on the nose.

The horses entered the start gate with me as nervous as the proverbial "whore in church." The gates sprung open and they were off! As they rounded the first turn my heart sank a wee bit because my horse was about fifth in a field of eight. On the backstretch, he made up some acreage and made the last turn third from the front. Feeling a little better I knew even in third place he would at least pay something back. Then the beauty of the sport began to unfold. The "field" started rounding the last turn. The jockeys with arms out stretched far enough to tickle their mounts ears, had me up screaming! In the last stretch, the long straight away which can last forever when your horse is behind, I believe my horse was stung in the ass by a bee. With an explosion of power, he kicked it in. In a few strides he passed the leader crossing the finish line. A winner by almost a full length. I felt vindicated and exhilarated over the fact my Uncle just won twenty-five bucks. I was jumping up and down screaming.

Uncle Stan being Uncle Stan nonchalantly congratulated me for my ability to assimilate and synthesize the information and pick a winner. I was excited I had won twelve dollars for every dollar he had bet. With a shit eating grin on his face, my uncle reached his half amputated index and full middle fingers into his shirt pocket and produced a ONE HUNDRED DOLLAR ticket he had bet on that horse.

If it were possible to shite me drawers at that very moment I would have! Instead, I grabbed that ticket like a "Willie Wonka Bar" wrapper imagining what almost twelve hundred dollars would look like. In a few moments, I stood at the cashier's cage and watched as the teller counted out the precise amount of winnings and hand it to Uncle Stan. For some reason, I already knew not to draw any more attention to us as he wadded the bills in a roll, shoved them in his pocket and off we went.

That night was Jim Beam shots and Schlitz around for Uncle Stan and my parents. For me? A Fifty-dollar bill was found stuffed under my dinner plate. And people wonder why I care less about the Lions and love the "Derby."

~#~

Uncle John was my dad's youngest brother. Quiet, shy and unassuming, this man proved to be a complex individual who endured more in life than many could imagine. He lived a life thinking his mother died to give him birth. Not true. He was born healthy and happy. It was my grandfather we would learn in later years who liked his Kessler's Whiskey. He wasn't a very nice man after he had too many shots of Kessler's. The story eventually came out that my grandmother found herself pregnant six months after Uncle John was born and attempted to abort the child with a coat hanger. Blood poisoning ensued; she died of suicide and not giving birth. A fact to be learned years later.

Anyway, Uncle John survived long enough to find himself enlisting in the Army after Pearl Harbor. Being the youngest, he was sent off to fight the "Big One," with so many other brave men. Germany was his theater.

As the story goes, he was separated from his platoon; two Germans gave chase. Obviously after two days, (remember now, these stories have as much credibility as a game of telephone with two tin cans and a string), Uncle John was exhausted and found a barn in the countryside, then hid in a hay pile. The German soldiers eventually found their way inside that barn. As the story went on, Uncle John prayed that if he wasn't' detected he would enter the seminary and serve God the rest of his life. He wasn't found. The two soldiers poked the hay with bayonets and satisfied there was nothing there, they left.

After the war, Uncle John tried to enter the priesthood only to be told his reasons for becoming a priest were invalid. I would guess according to today's diagnosis, PTSD would have been appropriate. Instead, he moved ahead, took a job as a city clerk in Detroit and eventually retired from that position. But that never stopped him from being an uncle.

He was my sister Chris' Godfather. He would come to dinner and spend time with my mom and dad at least once a month. And imagine MY surprise when he announced he had purchased a pheasant hunt for he and I at the Upland Hills Farms Reserve for my thirteenth birthday!

Extended family while growing up in Detroit meant being a family. I will never forget that hunt. We both killed a bird apiece. He didn't want to be bothered cleaning them, so he paid an extra FIFTY CENTS each and had the reserve clean them. I felt like the King of England on that hunt.

~#~

Aunt Toni and Aunt Catherine were the youngest and oldest of all the siblings on my mom's side. Always available to take me to Tiger baseball games, I spent many hours at the old Briggs Stadium every summer.

Back then the extended family was part of living. My aunts and uncles were granted the permission of discipline without recourse if we were to step out of line. We never did and they never found the need to dispense any discipline. Perhaps there existed a mutual respect?

As a kid, I had great role models; parents and extended family that worked hard and played hard. I have already told stories of remarkable memorable holidays filled with joy and laughter. But now allow me to share some other values I learned by example; the art of living outside of yourself! The ability to see is NOT always about me.

Maybe it came from a grandmother who at 13 was a stowaway to this country, who ended her journey here in Detroit never to return to Poland again. Or perhaps it was the fact she became a widow in her late 20's and raised seven children doing odd jobs and when the need arose, took in two foster children who became one with the family? I am not really sure when the lesson for giving started, but it does have deep roots in my family.

Maybe my role models learned to share out of necessity. Oh you know what I mean, the stories of walking 23 miles in the snow to school…both ways uphill! Or the Christmases where an orange was the only present; but share they did and it appears the greatest present they ever gave was of their selves. Let me give you a couple examples.

I was perhaps eight when my Aunt Toni and Aunt Catherine took me to the Starlight Restaurant in Detroit for breakfast. A quiet unassuming place; today well dated in fixtures but fresh and full of home cooked meals and many more memories. I remember we were seated toward the back and the table across had vacated to pay their tab. As the waitress began clearing plates of half-eaten pancakes and sausages, I noticed a dirty, disheveled old man stagger up and ask the waitress if he could have the leftover pancakes.

"NO," my Aunt Toni yelled! I sat there semi stunned wondering why my aunt protested the man take the leftovers. She had startled the other patrons and staff as well. The answer would soon to follow. "Sit down here," she pointed to the empty seat and ordered the old man into the booth. She began barking orders to the waitress, "Give this man anything he wants and LOTS of it and give ME the bill."

I sat in amazement watching him eat like I had never seen any man eat before. Eggs, bacon, sausages, pancake and coffee…lots of coffee. It was a chilly fall day and he cradled the coffee cup as if it were a campfire warming his hands. He was still finishing as we were leaving. My Aunt Catherine walked over to the table and tucked a ten, or maybe a twenty dollar bill under the man's paper napkin. Stunned he couldn't say a word. I walked away watching his eyes well up in tears. He mouthed a simple thank you.

A second story would be about my Uncle George. Uncle George loved to fish. I think he was the creator of the bumper sticker, "A bad day fishing is still better than a good day at work!" Uncle George fished mostly the St, Clair River or along Jefferson Avenue by the Belle Isle bridge. He always took two sets of matching rods and a duffel full of extra gear. I always wondered why his rods and reels were twins...then again came along my lesson.

An older black man sat on a weathered park bench fishing. His rod had a broken tip so the line was splayed out about four inches from that broken tip. The old and I assume rotted braided line was stuck in his reel in the classic "birds nest." Every time we hauled in a new trophy I could see the man watching with envy. He would reel in his line only to see that what little bait he had, was stolen by a hungry fish that was clever enough not to be hooked.

After a few hours, I watched as my uncle searched through his canvas duffel. He found a smaller canvas bag and began filling it. Leaders, line, hooks, sinkers, a new reel. He tossed in a pair of pliers and fish scaler to round out the rest of the tackle cache. He ordered me to pull in two of the rods and clean the hooks and pull up the basket full of the fish we caught. Carefully he folded the leaders he made into the brown paper bags, set the reels so the line wouldn't splay out, and then carried everything over to the man. I sat and watched as my uncle handed over perhaps a couple hundred dollars of equipment, 20 or 30 fish in a brand new basket and gave it to the man! For a kid growing up back then in Detroit, the memory of an elderly black man crying and hugging a 50 something year old white guy will leave an indelible mark on that kid's memory.

I never saw those men again. However, I knew at least on those two days someone had made a difference in their lives and at the very least I had to step outside of myself and at least honor the memory of my aunt and uncle who gave so much to so many.

~#~

I suppose every family has two sides. Maybe three or twenty-two; however, I would be remiss in talking about the "other" side and how growing up may not have been influenced by the Detroit culture.

You see, I am second generation Polish. That means my grandparents ALL came from the "old country" and discovered the "new."

Unfortunately discovering a new country does not mean the old adages, the old traditions and ideas were switched by landing on Ellis Island.

Long story short? My paternal grandmother passed away from sepsis attempting to abort her fifth child. My dad and two uncles were sent to St. Joseph's orphanage in Jackson, Michigan. (Their sister to a different facility somewhere in Detroit). Tom Monaghan of Domino's pizza fame allegedly spent a few years at St. Joe's as well. Here is the excerpt from the *Jackson News* updated July 7, 2017 and written by Leanne Smith:

"JACKSON, MI - Its most famous resident may be Tom Monaghan, founder of Domino's Pizza. But for decades, the St. Joseph Home for Boys helped change the lives of thousands of children who called it "the only home I ever knew."

The Home, as it was called, started in 1911 when the mansion of Jackson City Bank President William Thompson at 406 N. Blackstone St. and 11 acres surrounding it went up for sale.

The Rev. Joseph F. Herr, pastor of Jackson's St. Joseph Catholic Church, thought it would be a nice academy for nuns and told the Felician Sisters of Livonia so. They bought the red brick Victorian house and property for $35,000.

The academy opened in June 1911, but closed within a year because it was just too far from the motherhouse in Livonia. Almost a year later, the sisters opened their doors to 20 orphan boys and began the St. Joseph Home for Boys.

The Home, which accepted boys of all faiths, served both as a temporary refuge for those in need and as a permanent home for orphans, ages 2 to 14. The goal was to develop the whole child by providing religious, educational, personal and recreational opportunities."

Years later my dad would tell me of the days where they were fed meager rations, were allegedly molested by the nuns and actually thought the Ku Klux Clan was the salvation to their hunger woes. Yep the KKK held regular marches in that city; when they left, they donated the leftover box lunches to the orphanage. Think about it, the KKK donating to a Roman Catholic Orphanage.

Anyway, dad swooned over an opportunity to get a box lunch filled with a real sandwich, potato salad, an apple and a cookie. Evidently, the potato salad was so good my dad and uncles were willing to trade cookies for double and triple doses of potato salad. Now you might ask, what does some orphanage in Jackson, Michigan have to do with my being raised in Detroit?

My sister and I always marveled at how my father and his brothers would relish food. They spent hours nurturing a meal. In retrospect, perhaps they treated every meal as their last. So imagine me, the precocious ignorant young man who was tired of weeks of roast beef, or the fourth serving of beef that was dried out like hammered cat shit, revitalized by a creative mother who added BBQ sauce to make it palatable, announcing being tired of eating the same-o stuff saying, "I won't eat that shit no more!"

Now imagine a dad who spent eight years in an orphanage eating raw rutabagas dug from a neighbor's farm because the ten gallons of potato soup, made with ten potatoes was just never quite enough to fill the void in so many hungry children. What sort of reaction would YOU expect from such a man? Yep! He took after me like a tiger chasing a wounded gazelle. And when he caught me, I feared I was about to learn that the shit I called "shit" would never be served me again. Thank God I had a mother who already knew what had happened. Thank God I was smart enough to say I was sorry, to sit down and eat that hammered cat shit and actually say it was THE best-hammered cat shit I ever ate. THAT was what it was like growing up in Detroit. We never had the best, yet in retrospect, we had more than others; even our parents.

After that, I never said another word about food. I had realized even then, this chubby cherubic Polish kid was being treated in a way my parents never were. Never once did I complain about the dinner being served.

Actually, when my dad was on strike because of the Unions requirements, the "stipend" was never enough to cover household expenses.

I learned to enjoy mashed potatoes served with buttermilk. Bologna and onions fried in oil and ketchup added for flavoring. Polish rye bread was filler when dipped in the oils and ketchup and savored for pure flavor. Even today, those simple recipes were fed to my own children and greeted with culinary delight. Amazing what butter, onions, bread, and seasonings can do to inexpensive meats.

~#~

Detroit was divided in the '50s and '60s. Racially the division wasn't as apparent as in the late 1960s. Rather, at least amongst the whites, there were segregated lines between the educated and the non-educated. To have been fortunate to have a high school diploma qualified many for the burgeoning "engineering" jobs. My own father was lucky enough to have had an elementary education. He was qualified to apprentice as a "millwright" which placed him above most of the assembly positions. So you see, neighborhoods were not only segregated by color, they were segregated by ethnicity AND education. A high school education normally qualified a person for an office position. Anything less, even as a skilled tradesman, a person would have been relegated to the rules of the unions.

Back then there was no unemployment. The unions collected dues and then as the "brotherhood," provided incomes for members during layoffs and strikes. It was no wonder why back then Unions garnered so much strength. At a time a family needed help the most, they provided it. Today, we have unemployment insurance which hypothetically usurps the power and controls Unions once had.

The real irony as I look back was there really wasn't any prejudice regarding one's economic position.

The houses we lived in were essentially a reproduction of the next. Our parents socialized together, shared drinks and cups of sugar without any thought of pay back.

Perhaps the one "prejudice" was from religions. Then again, I stand corrected. Blacks did not live in my neighborhood. They lived in the areas where public transportation was easily and readily available. Blacks were relegated to the poorer areas of the city. I never saw a homeless person in my neighborhood. But I saw plenty in the inner city. When my dad was laid off or on strike, the neighbors would always be available with a pot of stew or soup. I was never cold. I was never hungry. I was always loved.

Exiting a bus in downtown Detroit, never failed to demonstrate the differences of the "we" versus "them." When my mom would take myself and my sister to Hudson's to shop and eat, I always noticed the women operating the elevators were Black. The cabbies were Black. The bellmen, Black. Where I was raised? No bellmen, no cabbies and certainly no elevators! It would be years when Northland Shopping Mall would be developed and there were no elevators that exceeded two floors. Escalators replaced elevators. Automatic buttons selected appropriately inside stores delivered us to the second, maybe even the third floors.

The ladies operating the old Hudson's elevators were always pleasant, congenial and smart. They always remembered your name after riding the elevator a few times. The men wore dark blue suits, white shirts, and ties. The women wore navy dresses with "doily" collars. They were all black. I suspect today, they were very proud of the jobs they held and did. They knew what was on every floor at Hudson's and could call out what we as shoppers could expect to find on each floor. Didn't matter. However, if you were looking for a specific item in the store, just ask the elevator operator. With great pride, they told you which floor, and then provided directions of where to find it on each floor. Again in retrospect, that elevator operator knew more about the store than many of the white managers did.

About that time A. Alfred Taubman created the "mall concept." Oakland Mall was his creation and it changed the face of retail. Eventually, the old traditions of shopping in downtown Detroit were replaced as the "malls" created convenience. We bought into the concept of our time was more valuable than yours, so convenience became synonymous with saving time. And since, in a city where the "assembly line" mentality took precedence over personal integrity or value, we began to buy into the fact we no longer needed elevators, we no longer required personal attendance. Instead, such a commodity created a completely new genre of entrepreneurs. We were actually led to think that such service was only for the elite, for the upscale, the upper end. The ones who now had college educations and could afford to pay for more. About this time, Oakland County, Troy, Birmingham, and Bloomfield became synonymous with affluence. Detroiters flocked to become one with the "in" crowd and abandoned their own roots.

Eventually, the Grande Ballroom, Olympia Stadium, Briggs Field (Tiger Stadium), Belle Isle, Boblo Island and the paddle-wheel boats that cruised hundreds of people to the island daily were all dry docked. They were no longer a part of traditions. They were lost along with Kresge Stores that became K-Marts. The Woolworths on Woodward that served hot waffles with vanilla ice cream. The Sanders hot fudge sundaes and Stroh's Bohemian style beer recently resurrected in the movie, "Shawshank Redemption," all lost to the concept of urban sprawl. To me it appeared if this sprawl separated and spread values. The family was no longer a unit. It was dog eat dog, every man for himself and the final nail in that coffin was the 1967 race riots in Detroit.

~#~

Nineteen Hundred and Sixty-Eight in Detroit, naïve once again; a white kid who has everything he ever wanted. Today it's named "privilege". I had no fucking clue what some inner city black kid had or endured living in the inner city. I just assumed it was always equal and level. Shit, Huntley Brinkley and Cronkite never said anything was wrong. Kennedy promised a lunar landing by the '70s and won. Race riot? What the fuck was that?

In high school, we had one Black girl. The conflict was she was born of two white parents. DNA tests indicated her great grandparents four times removed or some stupid shit like that believed one of her ancestors may have been of African descent. Students of DNA assert genes can pass a generation or two and then become dominant; a plausible explanation for me. I didn't care. The young lady was a real sweetheart. One of the nicest young ladies in our class. Yet, I can't imagine what it was like being raised by two white parents while I am black. Imagine further being a white male, married to a white woman and having a middle aged 1950s nurse, wearing starched whites with the perfunctory starched cap, enter the waiting room and ask you to come see your wife. Then, being led to the nursery to see the pink bassinets all decorated with storks and names, only to realize the one black baby having YOUR name on it, is your child. I bet there was a ton of explaining and research to be had. Gratefully, this young lady had loving, caring intelligent parents.

Eventually, the grapevine informed us of her story. I will never forget the prejudice that young woman graciously endured as part of a Catholic school.

~#~

Briggs Stadium and Detroit Tiger baseball. The smell of freshly mowed lawns; peanuts, popcorn, and Coney dogs. Barkers spent hours walking around carrying trays of watered down sodas, frozen ice cream sandwiches, roasted peanuts and bags of almost stale popcorn. I remember my dad saying he had to pee and always coming back with a cold Bohemian beer. Yep Stroh's that was later emulated in the movies "Shawshank Redemption."

Later in years when I was able to choose a beer? Bohemian Beer sucked! But in July at eighty degrees, a cold beer was like having sex on a deserted island.

It was the excitement of the time, the aura the ability to worship sports stars that we would never meet except for George Kell's and Ernie Harwell's vocal dictations of each pitch. (Yes in later years, people brought the old AM radios to listen to the Kell/Harwell explanations of each pitch, hit and play we all observed mere moments before).

After a few beers, diluted pops and melted ice creams, the "7th Inning Stretch" was always a welcomed reprieve. Except for my dad. You see, Dad thought ahead. In the sixth inning, he would run for a beer. Dragging me along, making sure we had our seat tickets we always managed to beat the crowds in the middle of the seventh inning.

I was always amazed at dad's ability to prognosticate events. For example, July was never a good time to visit the Detroit Zoo. Middle summer meant plenty of visitors. Also meant the prices were increased and hell, July was meant for BBQ's and the Fourth of July. Weekend baseball games were also off the radar. Night games were often more fun because they had fireworks. You get the idea.

But you see, my father also invented the concept of "crowd funding." Yep, he did. Every time at any baseball game the announcer would spew statistics about the game and the players. They would play that stupid organ music during pauses where the announcer lost his notes. But at the end of every Seventh Inning Stretch, there was always that attendance record; the count of how many people were there at the game.

It didn't matter if they were in their seats, ordering hot dogs, a beer or "relieving" themselves. It was the announcement of official ticket sales.

Picture this; "Ladies and gentlemen, today's attendance of loyal Detroit Tiger baseball fans is twenty-eight thousand, three hundred and forty-seven!"

Cheers would echo the stadium. I sat there stuffing my fresh "Ballpark" hot dog in my face and marveling at the crowds. My dad? My dad would look at me and say," Now imagine Jerry if everyone in the stadium gave you a dime!"

Thinking a moment I thought, "Holy SHIT!" I quickly multiplied the numbers in my head. Excluding my dad and myself, that meant I would have twenty-eight hundred and forty-five dollars in my pocket. My mind reeled at the possibilities.

What if I could get all the people to give me a quarter? Or what if only half gave me a dollar and the rest a dime? Oh my god, cha-ching! I was light headed at the possibilities. I was already leaving home and marrying Shelley from across the street.

And then the eighth inning started. By the ninth, I was content to eat the rest of the roasted nuts. The crowds were dispersing. But I never forgot about the possibilities.

Today we have computer sites that support crowd funding. Imagine if only ten million people gave you one thin dime!

~#~

Summers on Belle Isle: BBQ's, fishing, paddle boats, concrete fountains, a freshwater aquarium and red deer. The island was accessed from Jefferson Avenue. It was approximately one and a half square miles or some 985 acres. It divided two countries in the Detroit River, Canada and the United States. People who have never been to Detroit are always amazed to know that across the short distance of the Detroit River lays an entirely different country, diverse in ethnicity and culture. Canada was always an excursion in itself and was the beginning of my education to cultural diversity and the value of being a U.S. citizen when someone forgets their "green card." My grandmother never learned to read and was never declared a United States citizen. So when my family consisting of Busia, and Aunts Toni and Catherine, visited Canada on a Sunday outing, my grandmother appropriately declared she was born in Poland. Unfortunately, she forgot her green card. Yep, we were detained. I recall my mother begging Customs to allow my mom and dad to drive the four miles to my grandmother's house, find her green card and not deport her.

Back then life was calmer. The Customs agent sort of laughed and agreed. Within half an hour the appropriate documents were produced. My elderly grandmother was released and thankful. My family was calmed and we went on our way. Imagine if that happened today! We'd have a national incident!

So anyway, back to Belle Isle. As a kid, I wanted to see and explore everything on the island. I enjoyed the aquarium, the deer and the paddle boats. Fishing was limited to small inlets but produced the best rock bass fishing ever.

Blankets, beer, and BBQ! My dad was in heaven. My Uncle George always enjoyed the view across to Canada. My aunts and mom were busy either chatting or cooking. My sister Chris would either read a book or join in with my aunts. The island had a small pony ride where the owner would stick a red Stetson on kids, strap on toy six shooters and while the pony plodded a well-worn circle path, we could imagine we were chasing outlaws. I always knew if my cousin Bob was there, we were guaranteed a pony ride. I was jealous of the kid. I begged for the pony behind him because he became my imaginary outlaw. I would use one of my toy six shooters and shoot him. Maybe I had anger management problems back then.

After the pony ride, we always headed for the aquarium. I loved the aquarium. Fresh water fish were kept there. Being a kid who loved to fish I was mesmerized by the size of each fish. I dreamed of one day being able to catch one. So did Uncle George. The two of us stood with noses pressed against the cold glass and watched as each fat lazy fish gulped in fresh water to pass their gills and mock us as if they knew how very safe they were there. In between the rocks and stones used to create a natural effect were also huge crayfish, some turtles, and frogs. My imagination would go wild thinking of the possibilities. After a huge lunch, my parents, aunts and uncle lazed on blankets settling pounds of ribs, potato salads and cole slaws. Bob and I would search the river's edge for frogs and turtles. Had I a slingshot in my hip pocket I could have pretended I was Huckleberry Finn along the Mississippi. My sister Chris was always designated as the babysitter while the adults sat quietly or napped. Neither Bob nor I ever saw anything as huge as what we saw in the aquariums, but the satisfaction of capturing an elusive frog or turtle was enough to make a good day great.

Eventually, the day waned, the adults gathered lawn chairs and grilling equipment to store in the old trunk of the fifty-five Chevy. Bob and I mercifully although reluctantly released the turtle or frog we prized. Belle Ile already began to empty of the weekend warriors gathered to enjoy the water and the amusements. A few drunks always stayed. They never bothered anyone, just stayed. It was assumed they found some small secret hideaway near the woods or a part of the secluded areas on the gold coast where they could be left alone.

As everyone packed the gear and eventually themselves into the old steel hull of the Chevy, there was a quiet; a sense of regret because the day was ending. Now I understand my dad was the one who suffered. A few beers, fresh air, some hiking and swimming and while everyone dosed in the old car, he had to stay awake and get us home safely.

On the way off the island we would pass the Detroit Yacht Club or the island's casino, the water fountains we had already visited. We never missed the chance to stop and visit the glass conservatory. I learned to love the conservatory. The freshness of the dirt and plants they grew there, circled by walkways sided by benches hidden under the flora. After I reached a ripe old age of eighteen, the conservancy was a destination I enjoyed taking a date. Romantic and inexpensive.

Eventually the island hosted the Detroit Grand Prix. It never really caught on at the time. Perhaps with the advent of the city emerging from bankruptcy and the State of Michigan accepting the responsibility of the Island and making it a state park, the golf course, aquarium, conservatory, zoo and even the Grand Prix will return. The park fees will be used to renovate buildings and the sites. However, I doubt the homeless will be granted a lifetime camping pass. Sarcasm intended here.

I should mention my dates at the conservatory. Saturday or Sunday afternoons at the conservatory were always a great day date. Parents loved me for it. Pick up their daughter at noon with a promise to be back before dark. No worries of some pimply faced kid taking their daughter to a drive in or a place to watch submarine races. So after her parents were assured I was safe and all was well we, would make a few stops along the way at favorite Polish bakeries, a Kowalski deli and some local beer store for pop. The drinking age wasn't eighteen yet so beer or wine was not on the menu. However, mattered not the season, the conservatory was a great date place. A winter picnic was always a perfect idea. Warm, sunny with a small trickling fountain and a real absence of anyone else made it a great opportunity simply to be on a date; a different kind of date that many of the suburban ladies would never experience.

I was grateful to have known that island. Besides pretending I was Huck Finn as a young lad, I could also pretend I was a sophisticated European tour guide as I matured into a young man.

Unfortunately, Detroit's ethnic and cultural atmosphere was slowly lost after the seventies. With the loss of diversity and the deaths of in my family, such trips and excursions became fewer and fewer. Many of the islands pearls and gems were lost to urban sprawl. Trips to Belle Isle eventually stopped. But the memories were never lost.

~#~

Rouge Park. A municipal park created by the City of Detroit. Rouge Park golf course. Rouge pools. My father and uncles all said they remember trips to Rouge Pools. Rouge Park was the premier place where families who refused to drive to Belle Isle could enjoy the "wilderness" of the city.

Pools, golf, driving range, tennis, toboggan slides, ice skating, shooting ranges including archery, for a plethora of activities for every Western resident of Detroit. Recently it was discovered the park even hid a nuclear launch site for warheads. Yes, warheads. The Cold War drove many to dig optional basements. I wonder how many more would have considered that option had they known?

The Wayne County Sherriff's kept their horses there for the Mounted patrols. The shooting range was used to qualify all the local police officers. I can remember hearing the shooting like it was a part of having Kellogg's corn flakes for breakfast.

Recently, there was a news report saying parents were incensed that a family allowed two siblings to walk a mile home alone. WAIT? A mile? Have we been frightened so bad that we cannot allow our children out of our sight? Is this the new definition of "helicopter" parents? From where I lived, the edge of Rouge Park was perhaps a mile. To the pools or ice-skating maybe a mile and half or more! And we walked that often during hot summers to swim and cold winters to skate. We enjoyed the benefits of all the park offered, we had to walk at LEAST a mile or more; ALL of our parents knew where we going and with whom. Perhaps the only ride we had was later in the evening after skating long hours one parent was elected to drive us home. That parent was usually the one who enjoyed skating as well and was glad to be there.

Now here is a great irony of my growing up in Detroit. My mom insisted my dad build a back yard skating rink so I could skate in the yard so if something happened, she would know where I was. Could this be the beginnings of "helicopter mom?"

The irony? The back yard rink was incredible. Every night it was flooded and the ice was smooth and shiny. For the postage stamp sized yard there was plenty room to at least host a third sized ice hockey rink. Friends would come over and we practiced our shots on the one kid willing to "sit in goal" and risk a loss of teeth and black eyes. Most often it was Joe who went long in the fall and caught the winning pass. He gained enough confidence or else he was hit in the head so many times with hockey pucks, he was either a brave warrior or lost any sense he had left in his head.

You have to remember. We were middle class. Most of our sports equipment was old hard balls wrapped in black electrical tape, used ice skates that we saved up for weeks to have sharpened and a couple of old LIFE magazines wrapped around shins, held in place with the same electrical tape or confiscated rubber bands. We never had helmets let alone a mask. Joe's dad added "wings" to Joe's hockey stick to create a pseudo goalie stick. We were forced to be creative, inventive to make do with what we had. We learned that from our parents who did things like add extra potatoes and water to stretch soups or use aluminum foil on old "rabbit eared" antenna to improve the black and white television set for better reception.

So anyway, back to the back yard skating rink. My sister Chris and I had to take turns. She and a friend or two would skate and pirouette wearing the tightly laced white figure skates with "teeth." Took me years to figure out those teeth were for stopping. Hell when you wanted to stop you turned aside and "dug in." No toe digs for this dude. In addition, the girls always took yarn from their mom's yarn baskets and made a pom pom for the toe of each skate. Some even added a bell to the middle. Not sure if the pom's or the bells made them skate any better, but they sure looked good. Then one day this kid from another school showed up with his black figure skates and black pom pom's on the toes. Ever wonder the reactions of a group of guys raised in sandlots would be to see some kid wearing shiny new black figure skates was? We didn't care. We had either no knowledge of human sexuality, didn't care or paid no attention. Just know that kid could skate and ALL the girls wanted to skate with him. Not the Neanderthals with LIFE Magazines stuck to their shins. Make no mistake, we all stood on the ice watching this kid skate with the girls we all wanted to skate with; we were all envious. Never knew what happened to this kid. Never ever found out his name. But I will never forget him.

  Having a backyard skating rink took work. It had to be flooded every night after scraping off the ice and snow. One particular morning after a good snow, I was busy scraping off the ice with my imaginary Zamboni; a fourteen-inch aluminum snow shovel beveled at the top to toss the ice and snow forward. I had already made a few passes across the ice. I was thinking I was close to spraying a light coat of fresh water to fill in the cuts and blade marks but, decided a few more passes with the shovel were needed to clear the ice. That was when my mother's helicopter theory came true.

The snow shovel snagged on a small crack in the ice. I had decent momentum going to push the snow, but this snag stopped me cold. On skates, my upper body stopped dead. My legs wanted to keep going. I was pushed backward on my ass. Unfortunately, my right leg twisted under me. I sat down on my right leg with the toes faced in the wrong direction. I actually heard my shin bone crack. Lying sprawled on the ice, all I could think was, "Shit this hurts."

Tears festered and froze across my cheeks. My mom was home but to call out was fruitless. The doors and windows were sealed shut tight against the winter weather. Thankfully a friend walked past, (we lived on a corner lot), and saw me lying on the ice. She called out over the fence and asked me what was wrong?

"Broken leg I think," came my pained reply, "please get my mom." I felt my shin. That lump shouldn't be there. Mom came out and slid her way across the ice. She wasn't a doctor, she was a mom. When she lifted my blue jeans up, the panicked look panicked me. The pain had dulled. My body's natural morphine was kicking in. I was more concerned how I was going to get back inside the house. My mom would not be a good poker player. Her poker face showed nothing but worry and concern. Guess her premonitions were real. Mom feared I would break a leg or get hurt while at Rouge ice-skating. Instead, I had a major fracture sustained in my own backyard. Dad was upset because Saturday he had a bowling tournament and now he had to take me to the hospital.

~#~

Dad loved bowling. He rarely watched baseball; enjoyed football when his teams were playing. Don't ask me who his teams were. I have no clue. I think he liked the Lions. But bowling; oh Lord, how he loved bowling!

Saturday afternoons or Sundays were spent watching bowling. Now understand, for my dad that was exciting. For a young man wanting to experience life, watching bowling was more like watching a worm trying to dig a hole to hide. For me? I was the kid who dug worms to fish. Now that was exciting.

Worm hunting, by the way, was a true science. It took true talent to produce a five-pound coffee can full of worms for a days' worth of fishing. I was the genius or worm hunters.

The process was easy, the capture required skill, prowess, and desire. Catching a night crawler in the middle of the night, stretched out in uncut Kentucky Blue meant one needed nimble lightning fast fingers. Pull too hard and that fucker would split in two. Not entirely a bad thing, just bad enough to know it wouldn't be baited on tomorrow's hooks. Worms I have been told knew how to regenerate. So I always assumed that split worm eventually healed and became whole. No matter, I still tossed the other half inside the can. Never once was I able to discern the difference or demise of some half night crawler.

For the uneducated, the unskilled, or the Neanderthal wanting nothing more than some pigskin review, catching a night crawler was a ballet of its own. See it this way. If you thought your next meal was predicated on your ability to catch a slimy ground crawling grass dweller, just how selective and careful would you be?

Here was the "drill." Water the lawn, soaking it to almost flooding. Let the moon set. Daylight or any light made night crawlers sensitive. Guess that was why they were called night crawlers huh?

So, the lawn is watered. Night has fallen. Crickets sing. No frog sounds. We didn't have frogs in the city. At least not the city where I lived.

Mom and dad sat on the porch while I prepared for the hunt. Flashlight with new batteries? Check!

Five-pound coffee can filled with top soil, leaves and bread crumbs? Check! (Allegedly bread crumbs fed worms. Don't ask me. I still don't know). That was all we needed to catch the elusive "crawler." And I was good. Oh yeah, I was rated an "EXPERT" at night crawler production.

Here's the secret. You know how the old flashlights always illuminated in "rings of light?" Oh yeah shit! You are used to the halogen and LED lights. Those lights focus directly. The old lights created a "halo" effect. LED's and halogens would suck today while hunting night crawlers. It's no wonder the new night crawler hunting technology is based upon strumming a piece a wood in the ground, causing vibrations to piss off the worms and make them surface.

See it this way. My parents watered the front of our house. Now I realize they did so because as I "hunted" worms. They could watch over me. I would start at the corner of the lot and make passes like a pilot spraying DDT. Except, I didn't make noise. I stalked the elusive "Night Crawler" with independence, with resolve, with commitment. Flashlight fixed next to my left ear, the grass still dewy from the watering was scoped with each step. Night crawlers were slimy. Brown bodies that sparkled were obvious in the light. Must be why they hated the light?

Slowly I stepped inch by inch, but slowly. I never turned. My eyes were peeled for the contrast of green grass, black soil and brown slime. I never searched the areas lit directly by the old flashlight. I always looked ahead to the haloed rings that were precursors to each step. It was there when the elusive night crawlers were found. It was there when a firm grip and pinch of that subterranean prey was caught. It was then when a firm hold around that slimy bastard would prevent him from sliding back inside the hole. They always fought valiantly but eventually they would tire of the struggle surrendering to my hunting prowess. I held him up in triumph pointing with the flashlight. Me ma and me da on the porch looked on nodding in approval. As I shined my old light on the wiggling prey still between two fingers. He fought courageously to get back to the earth so he could hide. Instead I dumped it into the coffee can with the rest of the victims.

Satisfied I was a hero, a warrior, and conqueror, my attention returned to the hunt. Stealth was important on a fifty-foot lot for night crawlers. If that site failed, there was always the neighbor's lawn. The issue was simple. Did they water that day? If not, then a hunt was fruitless and the thought of spending a buck and half for a dozen night crawlers would become obvious. That is why a good, no, a GREAT fisherman always had a backup plan. Dad had buried an old wooden box in the ground. Tonight's night crawler haul would be deposited back inside the earthen cage where we fed them with grass and bread crumbs to await their fate at the end of a barbed hook.

Let's be realistic here. They certainly were no martyrs. Their soil was tossed and turned with apple cores, celery stalks and old heads of lettuce. Their left over castings were used by my mom for fertilizers in her flower gardens. And the fish we caught were our own rewards on Friday Night fish fries!

Shit! Back to bowling.

Crown Lanes on Plymouth road was my dad's haunt along with the Redford Lanes on Grand River and Beech Daly roads. Here are a couple observations/questions: When I was growing up, bowling establishments were called "alleys." Was that because they were back room establishments that only a few dared go? Or because the long wooden and well-waxed floors led to some dark alley where a kid known as a pinsetter sat and replaced the pins you knocked down as well as the old hard rubber ball you used to defeat the wooden pins? Or, was it because technically, for every bowling league, there were "jackpots" that were technically illegal and there remained the old seedy resemblance of a backroom alley speakeasy?

Who knows, who feckin' cares? Every morning, afternoon and evening there were men's leagues, women's' leagues, and "mixed" leagues. On the quiet Saturdays, a children's league was where frustrated dads could take their kids under the pretense of a family outing. Except in me Da's case, he was there because he wanted the chance to sharpen his own bowling skills.

That WAS how Detroit rolled in the '50s. The sixties were not much different. By the time the '70s arrived I was too "cool" to bowl with dad and joined my own league. Regardless, I actually recall some old smelly oily bowling alley where the wrought iron ball returns scratched the fuck out of your bowling ball; where some slim Pall Mall smoking kid stood spread eagled at the back of the lanes waiting to manually drop pins into the pinsetter so he could sweep away the "dead" pins, and people waiting for their bowling ball as it chugged its way back for the next salvo. Eventually the pinsetters, wrought iron ball returns and table top score cards were replaced by the new innovative, automatic pinsetter and ball returns with overhead lighted score cards. Those lighted score cards became like a fire in the woods. Teams of people stood with heads up staring at the scores of their competitors, swilling more Bohemian style beer. For many, a Tuesday night bowling league broke up what was often a monotonous long week.

Interesting isn't it? We bitch about technology replacing jobs today. Tell me what an uneducated kid of the fifties did when his job was technologically replaced by automatic pinsetters and ball returns? How did he/she list his skills on a resume? "Creative and experienced pin-setter at XYZ Alleys where I would move a pin over an inch or so to help the poor slob make an impossible spare and make him a hero."

If you think that shit didn't happen, then ask some seventy-year-old tattooed man who worked that job. The problem is you would probably have to visit some Veterans Hospital to find such a person. Honor and integrity went to war. Pompous bullshit became a second lieutenant who only had enough balls to add a tattoo in a drunken state, much to the pain and tears of some upper middle-class mom and dad who never figured out where they went wrong. At least the tattoo had the inspirational inscription, "I Love Mom."

Imagine if some pimply faced asshole from the '40s or '50s came home with a tattoo emblazoned on a taught bicep that read, "Tatyana FOREVER." Probably why so many women in the fifties and sixties excused the need for stress or diet pills? I mean. Why accept responsibility for an unruly son, a daughter sent to a "Catholic" school for wayward girls or a husband banging his secretary? The fact that mom burned a frozen dinner? The Twin Pines milkman was smoking hot, or the fact that dildoes were not yet available with batteries? I am sure we can place the blame on technology replacing pinsetters, dial phones, vinyl records and AM radio as well.

Looking back on this chapter on my Dad's bowling, I realize I didn't say shit.

But bowling on television was eventually replaced by the concepts of expansion sports teams. The late sixties showed an increase of hockey team growth from like six to twenty. A season of some fifty games to over one hundred and fifty. The television stations figured out their own math. A million viewers as potential customers for cars, clothes food or whatever, was easily parlayed into advertising costs per minute. We didn't have pay for TV then. The stations made money, LOTS of money selling advertising.

A Thanksgiving Day rivalry for Detroit's Lions in the sixties was a religious experience. But what was a six game season had been replaced by an eleven game season, with an addition 23 kabillion playoff games culminating is something called a Super Bowl. Please forgive me. With a football season that starts in July and ends in March, when would we expect our kids to play street football before the streetlights go on? And think of the revenues for all those ads!

For that matter, Life Magazines for shin guards have been replaced by exhausted parents driving the hockey circuit to be sure their kids got "ice time," and spending thousands of dollars in gas, equipment, and hotels; just to be sure "Johnny" has a chance to compete. Best equipment means best performance right? I think not. But hey now, Little Johnny looks fucking awesome on the rink yes?

Add in "Sally" being able to compete with all the boys. The reality TV shows create shows that depict frustrated parents being told their kid isn't shit at the sport, then going ballistic at the coach or whoever, while their kids sit in the back seat of a "grocery getter" playing video games. Sells advertising though doesn't it?

Sorry. The fifties and the sixties may not have been better. But they were easier. My Dad bowled and even though I thought he was a nerd, I still loved him and respected him. He took time away from his bowling to take me fishing or my sister to the movies. He was a talented and inventive man who didn't need to spend money on me to show me his love.

My mom didn't use diet pills or drink or worry about me beyond my trips to Rouge Park skating. At three o'clock every day she would put on makeup, lipstick, chill a couple beers and be sure dinner was ready. Even more important for me was the example my parents set. At almost 3:38 pm every day my dad would come through the side door. At the top of the steps stood my mom, fresh makeup, new lipstick and a change of clothes.

I never doubted their love. I experienced it, every day. Mom would toss her arms around dad's neck and kiss him. Dad would pat mom's ass, toss his lunch bucket aside, and me? I sat there watching content and happy. They loved each other. Why would I argue with two people who asked me simply to be home, when the streetlights went on?

~#~

Sears, Federal and "Monkeywards"

Retail shopping was quite strange growing up in the fifties and sixties. It wasn't necessarily a social event. It wasn't one of those current "Black Friday" events where people stampeded into a Target Store to save money. Don't get me wrong, people always love to save money. But back then we shopped. We took time searching and looking for that one perfect gift. We weren't driven by price tags, Disney or a child's psychological welfare. We bought pajamas, slippers and a toy. Come to think of it...maybe the psychological welfare of our children was their own assurance they would be warm at night, have food and be loved?

Alfred Taubman was the precursor to the new modern shopping mall when he opened Oakland Mall. I wasn't impressed. Allow me this, I may not now, was not then, and will never be a consumer. The ONLY reason why I stopped shopping online is that I have recently had my personal email hacked. A few hundred dollars later I have online protection and an absolute fear someone or something lurks outside the parameters of "techno world" wanting a piece of my ass. Or maybe a phone number and a social security card number. Never really mattered much; back then credit was paid monthly. Cash was king.

Speaking of technology, as a kid the closest thing we came to owning a cell phone was two tin cans, a hole poked on the bottoms and a length of string tied between the two. As far-fetched as it may seem, one could talk into one end and the other as the listener would hear what was being said. We discovered the quality of twine, probably because it could vibrate at the frequencies of the spoken word, improved the quality of communication.

I myself being the skeptic I am, decided the string had nothing to do with it. I was thinking two people ten feet apart could hear what I was saying at any level just above a whisper. (A whisper didn't really work into a tin can).

So I decided to experiment. Forty feet of my mom's best wrapping twine she absconded from my uncle's butcher shop; two freshly washed Campbell soup cans and a willing friend to help. We stood on my parent's front lawn, stretching a forty-foot string attached to two tin cans talking like we were miles away on a telephone. Damn, it worked!

I was delighted, my friend was nonplussed. He insisted we take turns speaking into the can on one end at varying levels of volume to see if the other could hear. I guess we never considered any hearing issues or loads of sand in our ears from the previous baseball game, collected by sliding into home, but damn it worked!

As we began to lower our voices to see if our words were audible, we also changed our words. A hello became," Can you hear me now?" Can you hear me now to, "Are you there?" Eventually, as our voices were lowered to a level we felt safe nobody could hear us speaking into a can...favorite explicatives took over; "You're ugly," became "Eat shit," and the final big one that always made an adolescents heart skip a beat with excitement because they said "that" word? "Fuck you!" We laughed like hell on that one.

Technology in the fifties and sixties was so much simpler. Yep, two tin cans connected with some bailing twine was never known to cause cancer. Well only if you ate the lead used to seal the cans. Television was available only on scheduled hours. During scheduled shut downs, we played games, usually outside. Parents rarely allowed us to use the telephone. I think we were charged a "user fee". So we ran over to a friend and yelled their names. But the things I learned about radio and television communications were the concepts of anodes and cathodes.

Our old black and white "Dumont" console, shrouded in REAL maple and "pickled" a creamy blond, was an exploration of wonder and intrigue. Those old televisions NEEDED a back cover to hide the fluorescence of the tubes inside. Each tube held a filament that lit like a bulb and with maybe a dozen tubes inside, one could actually do their homework by the lights! So they always manufactured a pressboard cover to shade the shine. The heat those tubes generated I am sure saved on winter heat bills and it was actually so intense, the manufacturer engineered openings to allow air to circulate and cool the device.

Usually below the screen in front, a piece of cloth kept an enormous speaker clear of dust. The quality of that speaker was at times less desirable to the sound quality of the two tin cans with string.

Back to those tubes.

You see an object as simple as a burned out television tube turned into an adventure. A chance to bond with my dad in more ways than one. In the old days, repairs of technology were my dad's responsibility. NOT because my mom was inept or incapable, oh no. My mom was a clever bugger. She knew taking a bag of burned out television or radio tubes to be tested was a bonding opportunity for many sons and their dads.

Cunningham's was essentially the only pharmacy/make-up/hardware/food/automotive/soda fountain store that was a precursor to today's pharmaceutical super stores. The only difference was the kiosk that stood conspicuously, enticing consumers to challenge their electronic expertise by testing maybe twenty or so allegedly burned out tubes. Not that it took a genius to test the tubes. You turn on the machine, plug in the tube in the correct socket, (there was a schematic for the patterns of the prongs exiting the tube; I suspect it was that way to drive the electricity to the tubes appropriately and if you didn't match the holes the right way, the odds of breaking off one of the fragile wires rendered the tube worthless).

Tube testing was a bit of a game for my dad. If he could determine a tube was bad, Cunningham's, of course, sold the replacements. If Dad could replace a tube at say three bucks, he could save maybe twenty-five for a TV repairman's visit. It was a game to my dad and technological game changer when it came to jobs.

Anyway, there stood dad and me, fitting tubes into the appropriate slots, waiting for the lights to shine in the filaments. No shine? New tube required. So for maybe five bucks dad fixed the TV. The old tubes, like light bulbs at that time were exchangeable. Dad and I bonded because he taught me what he knew about electronics, and at the time I thought he was an Einstein. He felt good saving money, I felt proud of me Da and grateful he had asked for my help.

With the low cost of tubes and the savings from not having to pay for the cost of a TV repairman, a trip to the soda fountain was guaranteed. Now understand, sitting at a counter sucking a soda was fairly common then. But, sitting there with your dad and talking shit about baseball or fishing or anything at all was worth its price in gold…even at today's prices of gold.

I mentioned light bulb exchanges. At one time you could buy a light bulb and when it burned out there was a one to one FREE exchange of every bulb if you returned them to any of the Edison retail shops. Light bulbs were another chance for adventure with dad; sometimes with mom too. The Edison store was near my grandmother's so when mom would take them it guaranteed a visit to grandma's house. If dad took them it meant a visit to the Men's YMCA on Clark Street to visit my uncle Stan.

I was always along for more than the ride. Many times bags of bulbs were handed in. Filaments never lasted long. The burn time may have been 40 hours so it didn't take long to accumulate burned out bulbs. Anyway, bags and boxes of bulbs were handed over at the counter and voila, a package of the exact same watt and quantity of bulbs were returned. Other stores would sell light bulbs, but they did not honor the free return policy. A monopoly even then, but I suspect at the rate of replacements needed, many people appreciated the free exchange, buying a bulb from the local A&P or Cunningham's was in emergencies only. Eventually, the free bulb exchange would end.

"This program, which had run for so long, was finally ended by one man: Lawrence Cantor. This man was a Detroit drug store owner who brought suit because Edison's program denied him the ability to sell light bulbs in his store. While he might stock them, who would buy them when they could get them for almost nothing from Edison? He filed an anti-monopoly suit in 1972, and the case went through the local and state courts, each of which sided with Edison's practice being legal, due to the permission of the Michigan Public Service Commission. However, the case was taken all the way to the United States Supreme Court, reaching this bench in 1976. Decided a couple of days after the nation celebrated its Bicentennial, in the case of Cantor

V. Detroit Edison Co. the nation's highest court decided against the Edison program, stating that acceptance by a state commission did not prevent antimonopoly laws from applying to it. The court ordered the end of the program, which came in 1978." ~Source, Patrick Bernhardt, Detroit History Examiner Blog, April 3, 2010

I was married in 1975 and frankly took advantage of all those free bulbs. Many of us who remembered the lines during the '70s gas shortage, relived those lines trying to get as many free bulbs as possible before the court order took effect. I think I collected enough to last at least a year.

To say growing up in the '50s and '60s was easier is perhaps a misnomer. Technology today has in fact lent itself to opportunities in leisure and travel. Perhaps the difference was more emotional. We had fewer choices leading to less confusion; therefore less stress. I can say, we were forced to look someone in the eye; had to face most people to share our thoughts and opinions. Even a telephone with the old party lines caused us concern about sharing or saying too much because if we knew who the other person of the "party line" was, they would know our business. If we didn't? God only knows who would learn of our lives. We really could not hide behind words that are sterilized by some electronic message where emotions are difficult to convey and misunderstandings great.

~#~

The "weekend." A weeks' worth of labor or school, study, and life, all culminated into Friday and Saturday. Those were the days when even when the game of hide and go seek was suspended.

Some other things you need to know about Friday nights in the city. Friday was usually "pizza night". Pizza delivery in thirty minutes was unheard of in the '60s. "Delivery in thirty minutes or less or it's free," was a marketing ploy successfully created by Tom Monahan at Eastern Michigan University campuses some time in 1984.

For the rest of us in Detroit during the '60s, a nighttime delivery of pizza meant a 6 PM order and at least a four-hour anticipated wait for delivery.

Anticipated, by the way, meant we were shipped a pizza that was reasonably warm and didn't need to reheat in our own ovens.

Friday nights were always the same with pizza. Cheese with mushrooms and pepperoni. I lived to past twenty before discovering one could order pizza with many different toppings. A friend's father opened his own sit-down pizza parlor. First time there I was mesmerized at all the choices in toppings. I was like, "No shit? All this for just a few cents more?" Onions, sausage, ham, bacon and double cheese added to the savory anticipation of each bite. And savory it was.

Extra napkins were always required to be sure the grease running down your arms never made it to elbows. Long sleeves were rolled up to prevent red grease stains from the selected toppings and tomato sauce. Never the less, a simple discovery of added toppings on pizza, later in life, became a simple delight!

Back to Friday night pizza; recall I mentioned we had to place an order early enough to assure it would be delivered at a reasonable hour. Before midnight that is. I can remember lying on pillows on the living room floor, Lone Ranger pajamas on, watching some guy named "Uncle Milty" and anticipating the familiar doorbell announcing, PIZZA WAS HERE!

Plates passed, forks for those needing them, perfunctory napkins and that succulent wedge of pizza dough slathered in tomato sauce, cheese, pepperoni, and mushrooms.

I think I just figured out why one reason I have always had weight problems. Pizza and the second Friday night selection, though NOT a second choice: George's Coney Island hot dogs.

People today think Senate or American Coney Islands are the best. Back then we didn't even know they existed. I mean they are in the heart of Detroit City and who would drive that far for a Friday night Coney Island hot dog when George's sat mere miles away?

For my family, George's on Michigan Avenue was the icon of Coney Dogs. Steamed buns, with a Hygrade™ dog, slathered in no bean chili, a generous "slide" of mustard on top and double onions; a gastronomic delight. Also a reason for antacids needed before bedtime.

Delivery wasn't available. Dad would slide into the old '55 Chevy and troop his way to George's on Michigan. He always ordered heavy onions, none of the Chicago Style stuff with kraut, pickles or tomatoes. My father was a purist; same dogs same toppings every time. Just like his pizza.

Anyway, the Coney's were double wrapped in thin sheets of waxed paper then carefully bagged in doubled brown paper sacks to retain their heat. Personally? I think they double wrapped them to retain their aroma! That '55 Chevy reeked of onions from Friday until Sunday's eleven o'clock mass!

Tomato juice; I forgot to mention the tomato juice. After a few beers, dad always finished off his dogs or pizza with a large glass of cold tomato juice and yep me too! Still enjoy a glass now and then.

It must have been those succulent chili soaked, onion buried and mustard drenched delights that caused my mom and dad to reminisce. Or maybe the combined aroma's brought back memories of the past. With each bite dad and mom shared stories about how George's Coney Island was forever the last stop from a date. Coney dogs with double onions and tomato juice. Come to think of it, it makes me wonder how my sister and I got here with all the nights of "onion breath".

I carried on the tradition of taking my future bride there after a few of our dates in downtown Detroit. The Old Shillelagh or Bob-lo Island excursions were always a great reason to stop at George's before our drive back into the suburbs. And no, the onion breath didn't stop us then either.

A last remark on George's. The place seemed to be frozen in time. The Formica table tops with the aluminum trimmed edges were there when I dated as when my parents dated. The only difference being the tables had been wiped clean so many times, the upper layers of Formica were worn down to the deep chocolate sub layers. The tabletops had edges that were distinctly original, while the centers were worn down from use. Waiters still wiped down the tops, shoveling food scraps into their free hand, simultaneously barking out, and "Two singles heavy, onions!"

Order pads were never used. Thin green three by five pieces of paper were dropped on top of the table, after adding the tomato juice or the occasional piece of lemon meringue pie. Never was there a mistake. Tips? Back then, in real silver coinage, was raked into one side of a split white apron the guys wore. One side for tips; one side for well-used pencils and receipt pads.

Highly efficient, gratefully familiar and always incredibly delicious, George's Coney Island was a mainstay along the Michigan Avenue corridor for years.

For me to sit there as a young man imagining my own father who at my age was there with my mom, was an enchanted memory.

~#~

Bob-Lo Island was a Detroiter's Disneyland. Old paddle wheeled steamers worked their way through the Detroit River stopping at Amherstburg, Ontario dock to pick up additional passengers, then eventually to Bob-Lo Island. I loved that Amherstburg stop. I watched as lines were tossed and the boats drew closer so passengers could come and go. Plus it prolonged the fun and excitement. Twenty-five hundred passengers were allowed on board. Music played by some three or four piece band. Kids played across the dance floor. Couples danced in the moonlight during evening cruises. It seemed there was something for everyone and parents gave us the freedom to roam and explore. I guess back then unless we decided to jump off, we sure as hell weren't about to get lost. And explore I did.

The SS Ste. Clair, (named after the St. Clair River), and the SS Columbia sat parked at the docks ready to transport eager passengers. I tried to position myself close to the rails so I could observe who was boarding. I don't know why. I just found people fascinating. Bob-Lo did not discriminate. Old, young, white, black, rich or poor, we all could not wait to get to the island of fun.

During the cruise, I sat and watched the wheels churn the water making that slap, slap, slap sound as each paddle made its turn around the red wheels. The engine rooms were exposed with glass partitions. You could watch the crew and the old diesel engine churning the drive shafts below decks. There was something hypnotic listening to the rhythmic hum of those old engines. I loved watching the engine crew. We weren't allowed in the steerage, but watching those guys operate below decks, constantly greasing and oiling was a sheer pleasure for a young man full of wanderlust. I used to imagine I was on a trip to anywhere but home. The St. Claire or Columbia was my vessel, my ticket to freedom and I was their captain. Besides the occasional muskrat that met their unfortunate fate either by the sweep of the paddles or some natural disaster, the experience was never marred by anything unpleasant.

    The old boats passed freighters, who blew the ships horn to the delight of passengers. Often the crew of these freighters lined the rails to wave at all those willing to wave back. It was then I learned the saying, "Red to the right when returning from the sea," meaning for those freighters inbound the red buoys were on the right side of the ship. Later I was to learn that right was "starboard" and left was port. Now that I am older, I think the port should have been the right since port wines are usually reds. There is never a time when I see a red or green buoy that I don't silently repeat to myself, "red to the right when returning from the sea." I just can never remember if port if left or right. Which I suppose poses another question. Are the buoys the same directions in the southern hemisphere? When I was seven years old I didn't give a shit. I was floating down a river, heading to a place where I knew bumper cars and caramel apples were limitless. My mom, dad, aunts or uncles allowed us the freedom to discover; to be a child with very few or no restrictions. Never did we think of the dangers to the innocence of childhood daily read about today.

No longer operational for some 35 years, the memories will remain for a lifetime. Never a summer passed where at least one and probably two excursions down the Detroit "Nile" found families in a place full of carnival rides, cotton candy and every imaginable sugared food created by man. Bob-Lo was a place where to a small child looked like heaven. To my parents?

Probably a days' worth of hell but my parents always endured. Plus if my parents wouldn't take us, I always had my Aunts, Toni and Catherine to take us. I doubt they liked the island as much as I did, but the hour plus riverboat ride never lost its appeal.

~#~

Paczki (pronounced "poonch-key").

I certainly would be remiss as a Polish Catholic if I failed to mention the "Fat Tuesday" tradition of consuming paczki's. A paczki can be defined as a half-pound of dough, built with two egg yolks then filled with the most exquisite fruit, cream or custard fillings. They were created for only one reason, to celebrate the beginning of Lent by imbibing with the decadence of a sweet calorie loaded pastry. Like "Mardi Gras", eating a few paczki's were symbolically the end of partying for forty days lasting until Easter Sunday.

Paczki is an experience. It is NOT a simple jelly doughnut. A dozen is at least fifteen bucks and six pounds of doughy delight. Eat one and you are full; then are drawn to slice open one or two left in the box wondering why that glistening sweet filling continues to call your name. Let it go, that guilt of diets and sculptured abs, won't happen. Lent is about sacrifice to the Polish Catholics. Paczki is about the debauchery before the sacrifice.

After "Fat Tuesday, (paczki day), comes forty days and nights of fasting, prayer, and more fasting. I remember my dad didn't mind the fasting part. What killed him were the "meatless" Fridays during the Lenten season. You need to know, my father was a meat and potato man. He could consume two pounds of pasta and with glazed over eyes search the table for the REAL meal. Meat!

My dad was funny about Fridays during Lent. He'd go to confession explaining to the priest that he was a hardworking man and after a weeks' worth of labor, a day without meat would leave him emaciated and weak. His arguments were always ignored and his pleadings were to no avail. Then one Saturday my dad flew red faced from the confessional. He never stopped to kneel for his prescribed penance prayers. He was sitting in the car before mom and I could make the sign of the cross. Once settled in our own seats mom asked him what was going on? Still fuming and spewing venom, dad went on to explain how he politely asked the Monsignor to extend a meat dispensation. I guess the Monsignor had the audacity to ask dad if he drank beer. Of course, he did. Every night. When the priest suggested dad give up beer for forty days, the Monsignor would excuse him from life imprisonment on the "meat rap." It was way too much to ask. By the way, a Monsignor is simply a higher ranking priest.

    Mom and I listened intently until he got to the part where dad swore the priest was grinning ear to ear when he suggested dad sacrifice the beer. His animated response made mom start laughing aloud. Dad shot me a look as if to say don't you dare. Sorry, I couldn't hold it in and in a few seconds, I suspect dad saw the humor in it all and he started laughing. The drive home was short and was celebrated by a cold Bohemian style beer in dad's favorite glass. He never did break meatless Friday requirements. He never stopped with his nightly "Bohemian's" in a cold icy glass either.

I should probably should mention, Easter season was not begun on Fat Tuesday. The next day was Ash Wednesday. That was the day to mark the beginning of Lent. Palms saved from the previous year's Palm Sunday were burned with the ashes used to adorn the foreheads of the congregation with a cross. It made me laugh. Some priest would make a thumbprint on one's forehead. Others would paint the sign of the cross as if they were Michelangelo painting the Sistine Chapel. It made no difference who applied the ashes. Those ashes either fell into one's eyes or were sucked into a nostril causing a sneezing fit. For me? I ran into the men's room and always washed it off. Some wore the ashes as a sign of promise and pride. It wasn't that I wasn't proud to be a Roman Catholic. I just didn't like ashes painted on my prepubescent greasy forehead.

Anyway, the season was marked by a change of color the vestments the priest wore. Purple was the choice with some parishes choosing to drape the statues and even the Crucifix above the altar. The idea was to remove the cloths on Easter Sunday to signify that Christ had risen from the dead.

Now allow me to explain my next comments. As a youngster, to me Easter meant a party at my grandmother's house. Food, baseball, cousins, aunts, and uncles; the entire family tribe gathered once again to celebrate, well, to celebrate family.

A week earlier we endured an extra twenty-minute gospel reading about the passion of Christ on Palm Sunday. Thursday of that week marked Holy Thursday in honor of Christ's Last Supper and to my dad's irritation another day of fasting. On Good Friday, everybody who could would file into the church to pray while Jesus was to have been crucified. Some even held the three-hour vigil of silence; another day of meatless fasting. Holy Saturday people would again attend church. For us, it was a day to color eggs and take the food to be eaten on Easter Sunday to be blessed by the priests and another meatless day.

Why the emphasis about meatless fasting Fridays during Lent? Recall my comments about "not eating that shit" and realize my dad wasn't fond of fish either. The thought of one day without meat was difficult enough, but three days? Unbearable! So here was dad's solution. Work all day Saturday. Come home and nap. Mom had taken my sister and me to church where a priest blessed the colored eggs plus hams, breads or anything else to be included in the Easter Sunday celebration. Understand my father's Easter Sunday began at the stroke of midnight. Therefore so did his meatless sentencing.

At exactly twelve oh-one Sunday morning, dad crossed himself and dove into a plethora of boiled eggs slathered in horseradish; pre-cooked ham, Polish kielbasa, and fresh rye bread also covered in fresh potent Polish horseradish which tinged the tips of ears with a pleasant burn. It brought deliciously wonderful tears to your eyes.

After about an hour of pleasure; one or more Bohemian style beers washed it down, dad was temporarily satisfied and ready to get some sleep.

Always amazed me how in less than eight hours he would repeat the ritual; then by three that afternoon again at my grandmothers.

Dad was never obese; hardly overweight. We just accepted the fact he didn't lie about his working hard and was justified in his quest to eat more than two pounds of pasta on Friday.

~#~

So there you have it. Four seasons of memorable events that marked my life. I have no doubt you have your own. Good bad or indifferent those memories, events, and circumstances are what formed our personalities and beliefs for life. Everyone has lived their own experiences. They established their own perspectives and created perceptions. The evolution of time through the seasons of a year and the passing in life is as different for you as it is for me. However, the one true memory, the one common denominator that appears to remain prevalent even today, is the one commandment issued by parents everywhere, "…to come home when the streetlights went on."

End of Life

By Jerry Pociask

"Death is not the end of life but the beginning of eternal life."

— **Debasish Mridha**

Copyright © 2017 by Jerry Pociask

This book is a work of fiction. Names, characters, places, and incidents are either products of the author's imagination or used fictitiously. Any resemblance to actual events, locals, or persons, living or dead, is wholly coincidental.

No part of this publication can be reproduced or transmitted in any form or by any means, electronic or mechanical, recording, by information storage and retrieval or photocopied, without permission in writing.

Walt stood patiently in line. The gift shop was very busy this time of day. Behind the counter a "pink lady" volunteer was dealing with a belligerent customer arguing the cost of some senseless plastic toys. The volunteer looked past the lady and smiled at Walt recognizing him as a friendly face. He smiled back showing his sympathy for the volunteer's situation. The other customer became louder and brasher in protest after her third credit card was declined. Waiting customers behind were starting to fidget impatiently. As the lady spilled her handbag on the counter in search of the needed cash to pay for the gifts; Walt stepped closer and tossed his credit card on the counter, "Allow me he said, it's Christmas."

Sheepishly the "pink lady" looked at Walt with somber eyes mouthing a quiet "thank you." Satisfied she met the financial requirements the customer left with dignity. Walt set his usual order of fresh cut flowers on the counter, and then counted out the cash from his pocket. He would have paid the ladies order in cash but he never planned for the extra expense. The credit card was easiest.

"Hi Mr. Hunt," Nancy greeted.

"Good evening Nancy…and please, call me Walt," he said counting out the $12.80 with tax.

"Yessir Walter! How is Mrs. Hunt," Nancy asked slipping the bouquet into the paper funnel alongside the register.

"Suze is a fighter Nancy you know that. She gets better and better every day," he lied.

Nancy folded and stapled the top of the paper funnel to protect the fresh flowers from the cold northern air. "Thanks again Walt, stay warm out there."

"Night Nancy, Merry Christmas."

"Merry Christmas Mr. Hunt, uhmm, Walt," she corrected herself.

The walk across the lawn was cold. Northern Michigan was beautiful in any season. But this Christmas Eve seemed like it was colder.

Bleak.

He hugged the paper funnel of flowers under his coat. The wind whipped and howled. So many times before he made this walk; and never had the flowers freeze or die. Human sentiments can be superstitious. Walter hugged the flowers like he hugged Suzie, tightly, protected, never wanting to let go.

She was his strength. "Why didn't I tell her that more," he asked himself?

Susannah was a few years older than Walter. Smarter, more experienced, or maybe none of the above. Gorgeous and beautiful and the moment he saw her he knew she was the one. The one who would always be "there" for him.

He couldn't honestly say the same for his being "there" for her. He always worked long late hours building his accounting business; never feeling truly adequate around her. But, he loved her to the moon and back. Being the quintessential hostess when they held holiday parties or entertained clients, no one ever left without total appreciation. She was a master chef, an incredible decorator and always coiffed to perfection;

perfect in his mind. Walt never felt he lived up to her standards. Their success was a direct result of his hard work and her ability to raise a family almost exclusively and remain as his stable rock.

Before Suze took ill there was never anything he went without. Now, his nightly visits, each new bouquet of flowers, could never equal what Susannah gave to him in life. It just never seemed enough.

Tonight he decided was different. Tonight he would tell her exactly how he felt. He would whisper his love, he would whisper her greatness. Finally, he would whisper his own apology for not being there for her, for his own inadequacies, for never having said, "I Love You!" enough.

She was his first love. His only love and tonight he was on his way to the ICU at the long-term acute care facility to wish her a Merry Christmas once again. Confused by life events, Suzie's mind wasn't as it once was, but tonight it was cancer that took its toll. Her mind was probably the same. Drugs, treatments and simple fatigue were wearing her down; and on him. Each day's visit seemed to tire him just a little more; not from physical exertion, but emotional. He hated seeing the once vibrant woman diminished to the trials of cancer.

Many times he begged and prayed to God to please give him this malady. To recognize the beauty of Suzie's heart, her love for people let alone the love she had for him and their children, but his prayers were never heard. Walter resigned himself to trying to understand the concept of "let go and let God." It always seemed to work those moments of justification, never in those moments when he saw how very much he loved her and how very much he missed her.

~#~

The automatic door opened with the same "whooshing sound" the old Star Trek television shows inserted when Kirk, Spock or Scotty approached a doorway.

The young face behind the desk was oblivious to Walt's arrival. Over the months, the facility never kept the same person. He just assumed it was because they never paid enough to keep personnel. Tonight the young lady looked up and smiled, "Hello Mr. Hunt, Merry Christmas!"

Half startled, half impressed, Walter smiled at the young lady with gratitude. "Good evening and Merry Christmas to you too, have any special plans with family?" he asked smiling back.

"Running home to wrap the last of the gifts while the kids are asleep; probably a glass of egg nog to relax before thoughts of Santa's arrival wakes the kids at 6:30" the nurse responded. Her enthusiasm reminded him of Suzie's, years ago when she wrapped gifts for the children.

The nurse continued, "Don't forget our Family Christmas tomorrow night," reminding him as he moved toward the elevator.

"Wouldn't miss it," he shot back, "Suzie's a cougar you know and with all these young men here I have to protect my interest in that gorgeous woman," then with a wink he pressed the elevator button, waited for the door to open staring at the lighted numbers counting down the floors.

~#~

He pulled the flowers from under his coat waiting for the elevator to stop at six. It moved slowly like the residents "Come to think of it," he thought, "he'd been moving slower these days himself." The doors opened on six, the nurses at the station always managed to greet the visitors with a smile and a friendly greeting. For some reason tonight he walked past unnoticed. He stepped into the hall leading to the resident's rooms. The entry was marked by a mirror with a table full of flowers; he stepped into the hall, checked his face in the hall mirror and chuckled at himself. The room was at the end of the hall giving him time to pull the flowers from the bag and refresh them, at the same time taking a deep breath to refresh himself as well.

~#~

Suzie's room was always cold, the monitors the beeps the smells, always the same. Walt detected everything "appeared" more acute this night.

Walt pulled yesterday's flowers from the vase and tossed them in the basket. The paper funnel from the new was crushed and followed. He took the glass vase to the bathroom for fresh water and slid the handful of flowers inside.

Again the door was pushed open, "Evening Mr. Hunt," the night nurse greeted him.

"Please, Walter or Walt. Whichever you prefer" he implored.

"Walter it is then," she corrected herself in an apologetic tone.

"Any changes," he asked.

The nurse held Suzie's wrist while reading her own watch, "Always changes Walter. She is a very strong determined woman. I suspect she is listening to us right now and thinking to herself she is ready to go home," she replied while plumping pillows and pulling up covers.

"Walt," the nurse's voice lowered with a trace of empathy "Are you doing alright? Are you taking care of you as well?"

Walt already knew, until tonight, he wasn't.

The night nurse checked the last few dials and buttons. "I'll leave you two alone. Merry Christmas Walter," was all she said and she was gone.

He rearranged the flowers, looked around the room wondering how she would want it to be.

"Listen," Walter started, "I was thinking it is kind of late so I may stay the night. That okay?" he asked the shift nurse.

The nurse tossed her shoulders, "Sure why not?" then remembered to add the last few entries to Suzie's chart. "Have a good night Walter." She left and dialed down the light of the room.

He stood quietly looking at his wife. A neon light over the bed dimly lit her face. He was grateful the light wasn't bright enough to show all the wires and tubes leading from her arm to all the bags and monitors.

~#~

Walt gently stroked her stippled red and gray hair. The cancer had taken its toll. A once thick long mane of red hair had rapidly lost its fiery luster converting to more of a wisp of thin gray.

The sounds of all the supportive machines seemed to diminish her very existence. Her breathing wasn't labored. She rested steadily. Her breathing matched.

Walt leaned in and kissed her. "I love you my Darling," he whispered, "to the moon and back, 23 kabillion times!" For a moment he thought the monitors changed their rhythmic cadence with his words.

Carefully Walt pushed Suzie's covers down and aside. Her thin arms were bruised black and blue from all the tubes and needles. "This must be what HIV patients look like," he thought.

No matter how hard he tried to liven up the room, the smell of death prevailed. Residents at a long-term acute care facility are usually not there long term and rarely leave by their own will. Walter looked around the room. Cards, flowers, and balloons adorned the walls.

He smiled at the one from Carrie, "Dear Grandma, I love you!" adorned in crayon scribbles.

~#~

The "beeps" and lights are terribly antiseptic he thought. They track one's life today without regard to the past. Interesting how we can live seventy or eighty years and be reduced to a blip on a monitor. She deserved so much more. The people who worked there were truly caring compassionate people. For that he was grateful. Yet, they knew nothing about the real Susannah; who she was and is. Perhaps it is better that way for the staff. They experience death and loss on a daily basis. It would be difficult always having to say good-bye to a new friendship made in only a matter of a few weeks. He glanced around the room one last time to make sure it was as she would have wanted. He knew the staff wouldn't be back for at least five hours to check on her, if at all since they knew he was staying the night.

The covers down, Walt crawled in next to Susannah. Adjusting a pillow and pulling the covers back up; he nestled and "spooned" his beautiful woman. His arm reached across to wrap her in his arms.

Snuggled against his love he felt secure. They had spent all those years together; similar goals, similar wants and similar needs. What would he do without her? Her breathing slowed when he hugged her. Her monitors relaxed. He pulled the covers up closer toward their chins. He nestled his face against her still soft graying hair. "A very strong woman indeed," he thought to himself recalling how red it was in times past, matching that fiery temper of hers!

Whenever she had her dander up he would always put on his "crooner face" and sing her the song that played at the end of the evening on their first date:

> Sunday, Monday or Tuesday
> Wednesday, Thursday or Friday
> I want you near
> Every day in the year
> Oh, won't you tell me when
> We will meet again
> Sunday, Monday or Always
> If you're satisfied
> I'll be at your side
> Sunday, Monday or Always

No need to tell me now
What makes the world go 'round
When at the sight of you
My heart begins to pound and pound

And what am I to do
Can't I be with you
Sunday, Monday or Always

Always and forever I must be with you
Beginning Sunday and Monday and then forever

Oh, won't you tell me when
We will meet again
Sunday, Monday or Always

If you're satisfied
I'll be at your side
Sunday, Monday or Always

No need to tell me now

What makes the world go 'round

When at the sight of you

My heart begins to pound, pound, pound

What am I to do

Can't I be with you

Sunday, Monday or Always

Now he moved closer to her ear and began purring "their song" once again, "What am I to do, can't I be with you Sunday, Monday or Always?"

~#~

Walt imagined Suzie heard his trembling voice singing what was to become their song performed on the evening of their "first" date; he hoped she felt herself sway in his arms to the music, "Always and forever, I must be with you…Beginning Sunday and Monday and then forever." He recollected her long red tresses gleaming in the lights of the Grande Ballroom. She wore a matching red dress; heels making her taller than her five feet six inches. She always assumed men were intimidated by her height; Walt tried convincing her most were intimidated by her sheer beauty. Long legs, long red hair, radiant smile and a wicked sense of humor were what drew men to her. He was no exception and he knew straightaway after he met her, she wasn't going to get away.

Walt watched her sashay a dozen dances on the well-oiled, slick hardwood floor of the Grande. He watched dozens of "hopefuls" ask her to dance, hoping to sweep her away; yet never, until that night did any man have a chance. He knew he was different, handsome, polite, charming, and confident; one hell of a dancer.

A mellow voice that could carry a note he did not have, but he loved to sing and she endured his singing while they danced.

He was also the first to ask to be granted multiple dances that evening. Recently inducted into the Army, he saw his life was charmed. His friends were shipped overseas, Japan, Guam, Germany. Fort Wayne and

Detroit were the hubs for every jeep, truck or part that was sent to the war effort. His "war effort" would be spent there in Detroit supplying the equipment for those men and women who were less fortunate than he. When he told her that, he noticed by her smile, she seemed to like the fact he wasn't going anywhere far.

~#~

Suzie's monitors seemed a bit out of synch a few moments which worried Walter.

"Oh my darling, how I so loved that song, and it mattered not how awful you sang it, I will always know it came from your heart, terribly from your voice, but always from the heart."

The monitors flickered once more and seemed to fall back to their usual rhythmic patterns.

~#~

The evening passed so quickly with the Tommy Dorsey Band; good music, great dancing. He noticed a slight bit of sweat on her brow. All that dancing makes one thirsty.

"Would you like a drink?" he invited. Suzie would have loved an ice-cold beer. She passed opting for an ice-cold cola drink, saying, "Feel free to have a beer yourself if you like." She wasn't opposed to having a drink. She liked this guy and felt maybe alcohol wasn't a good idea for now. Something about him intrigued her and she wanted to know more about him. But she didn't know him all that well and felt it rude to insist he not imbibe if he wanted. Her refusal to have a beer and yet offered him to help himself put his mind at ease; but he passed as well opting for an ice-cold Vernors ginger ale. She stood watching him as he paid for the drinks. Suzie always believed that the way a man treats "service" people, is a great indicator of how he would treat others, and she was pleasantly surprised he was a gentleman even when buying to cold sodas. He turned and offered her the cold drink with a bent straw.

She took a long sip and grabbed her forehead, "Whew, drank that too fast."

He smiled at her and grabbed a couple napkins so she could wipe the tear from her eye that formed from her drinking the cold drink too quickly. Gratefully she accepted and used it to remove the glistening moisture on her brow. He took a long draw on his own drink as well. She laughed as he grabbed his own forehead; she offered up one of the unused napkins. He accepted and cleared his own eyes.

After a slightly awkward moment, he glanced over and nodded toward an empty table, "Would you like to sit?"

"I would like that," she replied.

"After you," he held his hand out to allow her to lead the way. The tables were crowded and she was walking toward a middle table when he spotted the open table next to an open window. His hand touched her back to guide her, "There!" he declared, "by the window." Not too private but private enough where they could talk without needing to raise their voices, she preferred his choice over hers.

~#~

The monitors jumped erratically once again.

"You were the quintessential gentleman Sweetheart, perhaps a wee bit too smooth. I wasn't used to being treated in such a cavalier manner. I took me a few moments to realize you weren't just full of shite. I remember following your lead without protest thinking, "This guy is smooth." You didn't know I giggled to myself the whole time."

~#~

He pulled her chair out and made sure she was comfortable, then slid his chair around so he could sit next to her. He put his right hand on the back of her chair. She stared at her drink and toyed with the paper straw. He took a few moments to "take her all in."

"Beautiful," he thought to himself. He fought an overwhelming urge to lean in and kiss her cheek.

"Not yet," he told himself.

Instead, he started with small talk; asking her about her. Did she work? What did she do? Where was she from? They chatted and laughed for about an hour. Finally, he mustered up the courage to ask with a smile, did she like a man in uniform?

Her answer was obvious when her eyes lit. He knew immediately not only would tonight be the first kiss but within a few months, this gorgeous red headed angel would carry the surname of Mrs. Hunt. She asked him the same questions as he had asked her. She smiled when he told her his deployment was not only stateside but right there in the city of Detroit. His trade as an auto mechanic was much needed here for the war effort helping supply jeeps and trucks and eventually airplanes for the service men at the fronts.

After what seemed like mere moments, the announcement of the last dance of the evening was a ladies' choice and the song was "Sunday, Monday or Always." A few bars started. Walter sat motionless for that few moments of uneasiness thinking, "Will she ask me to dance?" Instead, she stood taking his hand, this time guiding him to the middle of the dance floor.

"Oh, won't you tell me when, we will meet again…" her eyes were hypnotic, she felt him pull her closer and this time, he leaned in and kissed her.

He walked her home that evening. He held her hand and they took their time walking her home. They had already made a second date. Standing in the shadow, just outside the glow of the light on her porch, he leaned in a second time to kiss her good night. "Good night Suze," he whispered.

She smiled at him. "Good night Private."

Walter fell asleep dreaming of that first kiss. He dreamt how passionately she kissed him back. The humming of each piece of medical equipment resonated in perfect unison.

"Oh, how I wished later that night we walked slower. I loved every moment of you. Your smile, your laughter and how you desperately tried to make me laugh with your silly jokes. No need, you made me smile and laugh the whole time. I no longer needed to hide my giggle. And finally when you leaned in to kiss me, I never felt a kiss feel so right; so warm and tender. You melted my heart and soul and I knew, "You were the one."

~#~

"Mr. Hunt... Walt, wake up please I need to do Suzie's vitals," the night nurse was waking him.

"She must really love you at her side; look at her smiling in her sleep!"

"Either that or she really *was* hearing the stories I have been whispering to her while she slept," he answered the nurse still wiping the sleep from his eyes.

"Stories?" the nurse asked.

"Suzie and I have been together for many years. We have had so many loving experiences; I just wanted to tell her how very much I love her and how very lucky I have been to have her in my life. So, I decided tonight was the night to tell her. I have been laying here sharing with her many of the wonderful experiences we have had together."

Half listening the nurse smiled, "get some sleep, Mr. Hunt."

~#~

"Good, the old cow is gone! Damn, I wish she wouldn't interrupt us. I was so enjoying our dreams together. Please go on my Darling."

~#~

Nestling himself back into Suzie, Walt whispered, "she's gone, love." Walt swore he heard Suzie sigh. Now, do you remember the night we went ice-skating? You were always so accomplished at whatever you did. That night was no different."

Walter whispering softly into her ear began telling "their" story. He was acutely aware her monitors responded to his voice. He continued to tell the story; knowing she heard him exhilarated him to keep going.

"The night was cold. Skaters circled the rink. You were in the middle doing your pirouettes and figure eights. I, on the other hand, clung to the side, step skating, hoping not to fall and make an absolute fool of myself," he chuckled.

"Do you remember love, the smell of coffee and hot chocolate at the concession stands, the sounds of laughter, the crisp cold; the cheap megaphone speakers playing Bing Crosby's "White Christmas" oh, how elegant you were skating in circles, your flowing red mane wrapping itself around your face as you turned!"

~#~

"I was trying to impress you. How could I forget this gorgeous sod of a man trying as he might champion the side boards lining the rink? Smartest thing you did was offer me that hot cocoa."

~#~

He went on softly whispering, "In mid-spin you stopped with one spiked toe and looked around for me. I had already left the ice and stood by the concession stand to order you a hot cocoa. All the men standing with me were mesmerized by your beauty, watching you execute swan-like moves on the ice. I did not have the heart to tell everyone you were a professional dancer; evidenced by long strong legs and athletic prowess. But it was that smile. Gleaming white teeth wrapped in thick full lips I had learned to savor with every kiss."

"You noticed me near the stand and stretched a skate sliding toward me."

"Gentlemen," I announced loudly to the outdoor crowd. "Do you see that magnificent redhead skating this way, the one who has mesmerized men for years with her beauty, the one who has demonstrated her athletic skating ability and now skates this way," I asked. "Eat your hearts out boys because that beautiful woman is with me and is mine!" "I swear Darling; to a man they were jealous of me and their dates and wives totally jealous of you." He laughed almost too loud, "And you? You blushed just like you always do." Walt thought he saw Suzie smile.

~#~

"I will never forget that night. No man had ever paid me such a compliment before. Here I was trying to impress you and instead, you stole my heart once again! I remember lying in bed that night never wanting a man as much as I wanted you then and there. And then? Then I cried because I was afraid I would never truly "have" you."

~#~

"I handed you your cocoa; after the first sip, you left a chocolate mustache over the top of your succulent lips. Taking your chin with my thumb and forefinger I pulled your face close to mine and kissed the chocolate away. I went to pull away; instead, you grabbed me tightly and kissed me deeply. Our tongues fenced; we nibbled each other's lips and lobes; I stroked and caressed your back wanting more, so much more. Later that night, we made love for hours.

Walt opened an eye when he heard her monitors jump. "I know my Darling; it was a magical night for me as well." He reached down and held her hand to his lips and kissed each finger. The monitor slowed when he placed her hand back by her side.

~#~

"WHY didn't you ask me then? Why didn't you tell me that night was so magical? Oh yeah, shit. The quintessential gentleman again."

~#~

Walt cradled Suzie all the while nestled contently against her pillow. Shortly he was again sound asleep dreaming; dreaming about their life together. The war progressed and it seemed as though our side was going to win. His job at the fort was getting easier and easier. It seemed less equipment was being shipped to support the war effort. It gave him more time to spend with Suze.

~#~

"I was never more relieved that when I realized you wouldn't be shipped across the pond. I had grown to know you, to see you as my one true. Had you left me? I would have survived, but I wouldn't have liked it."

~#~

"Once I saw you walk down that aisle love, my heart was in my throat. I will never forget how incredibly beautiful you were; all dressed in white a long flowing gown contrasted by your signature flowing red hair. I remember fighting back my tears of joy, which were lost as we professed our vows. I took your hand and placed that sliver of gold around your finger. Nobody will have ever convinced me then the value of what was to be a few dollars of gold could be parlayed into a rich lifetime of dreams, hopes, and aspirations. What a beautiful day it was as we married. Friends, families, music, and dancing; times were tough; neighbors brought food, alcohol, and desserts. Music was played by anyone owning an accordion, guitar and a drum. I will never forget the look on your face when the bagpiper arrived. Everyone looked over speculating what was to come next, yet they all knew to be soundless. The bag inflated and the steady hum of the pipes signaled a beginning. Then, the piper began playing Auld Lang Syne. Not a dry eye in the house least of all yours. That piper cost me two weeks' pay and based on your reaction? I would have given a year's pay. After dinner, the Wedding Song played. I led you to the center of the room. We danced and I sang to you,

> Oh, how we danced on the night we were wed
> We vowed our true love, though a word wasn't said
> The world was in bloom, there were stars in the skies

Except for the few that were there in your eyes

    Dear, as I held you close in my arms
    Angels were singing a hymn to your charms
    Two hearts gently beating, murmuring low
    "Darling, I love you so"

The night seemed to fade into blossoming dawn
    The sun shone anew but the dance lingered on
    Could we but recall that sweet moment sublime
    We'd find that our love is unaltered by time

    Dear, as I held you close in my arms
    Angels were singing a hymn to your charms
    Two hearts gently beating, murmuring low
    "Darling, I love you so"

Time has a way of erasing memories, thoughts, and voices. Try as I might, a voice again unable to hit the notes, becomes a memory and a wish one would simply like to say shut the fuck up! "You were absolutely beautiful that night Darling. I will never forget how you looked." Walter paused in his thought, "Come to think of it Sweetheart, you always are absolutely beautiful!"

~#~

"You never could sing. And oh lord, the hours I had to endure. Der you know you never could hit the notes? But to me, it mattered not. There was never a man who loved me as unconditionally as you. So I thought what is my penance? YOUR singing! A wee price to pay for such elegance as a woman could ever imagine."

~#~

A few hours later, Walt woke and quietly slid off the bed; padded out of the room into the brightly lit hallway and made his way toward the lobby. He passed the front desk and sought solace in a more private environment. The media room was mostly dark except for the artificial tree staff put up. The colored lights only lit part way into the room.

The leather chair invited him in. Gratefully he accepted, and the tree lights beckoned. The small table held an old Marantz stereo. He pressed the button; the station display opened to a plethora of stations. On this night he only wanted the station that aired only Christmas carols. Every year this station played carols starting in November and ending December 25th at midnight. "Too many choices," he thought to himself turning the dial slowly listening for Christmas music. Finally the sounds of Nat King Cole's "Silver Bells" filled the room full of holiday nostalgia.

Settling into the deep leather chair was more comfortable than the standard hospital-type bed; deep plush back and armrests eased the pain of past injuries. Tired strained muscles made Walt weary all this time.

~#~

"Go rest my Darling. We will soon be together again."

~#~

Suzie was first diagnosed over a year ago. He was glad he had already retired. After some treatments, they shared a trip to Hawaii. Yet each day after he saw her fade, the treatments only prolonged the inevitable pain. Her dancers step slowed. The long luxurious mane of red slowly fell and then returned faded, finally gray. The only physical aspect that never changed was the sparkle in her eyes. Even when in pain, her eyes smiled when he entered. Her eyes truly reflected her love and feeling for him and her family.

And now, even though he was tired, he was determined to remain strong for her. She deserved to know her life was not for naught. She deserved to know she was loved equal to all the love she shared; greater than the sum of her ability to love since she affected so many lives. She spent a life teaching her special kids with the now "politically correct" name of Downs Syndrome. She spent her life making sure the developmentally disabled had an equal "shot" at life; a life equal to everyone else.

Her mission led her down many paths and many adventures. One time she spoke of a young lad, Alex who was mesmerized by her beauty as was every other man. Upon her return from a one-week camping adventure, she spoke of Alex. A delightful young man who needed a quick story told every night before bed. Suzie's eyes sparkled while she told her stories. Seems Alex this day was a bit difficult. When it was time for "lights out" Suzie found him agitated. She half laughed and half cried telling her version. Alex was a full-grown man in a little boys mind. Suzie went on to say she told Alex his good night story; just as she was ready to leave, Alex told her it was alright if she chose to stay with him that night. He was alone, had been his entire life. Protocol dictated otherwise. Not that she would have stayed. Just, she knew that same loneliness. Walter recalled hearing her tell the story; as mesmerized as Alex that night as she tucked him in!

He thought to himself, "Her love radiated; rippled like that analogy of the stone tossed into a pond. The "event" to her was minimal, the effect she has on people? Profound."

~#~

Antiseptic aromas were inescapable in any medical facility. Any attempt to mask the aroma of human feces, urine and bleach were nearly impossible. Staff attempted to mask the odor in the media room with lit scented candles. During the holidays the fireplace burned much of the aroma away like a match hiding a fart. The fake trees, while beautiful, remained fake. The only redeeming quality was the smell of heated cider, fresh baked cookies and the glow of the hundreds of lights in the room. He stared at the tree and the gas logs in the fireplace. Old eyes with the beginnings of cataracts made the lights appear as stars. Christmas carols played softly on the radio; tired as they were, his eyelids slid down and covered the last remnants of old memories and any light.

~#~

"Kids, Santa was here!" He called out from the bottom of an oak stairwell. The garland wrapped banisters were lit by old-fashioned lights as was the entire home at Christmas. Brewed coffee, with sweet pastries, filled the old Victorian with the most wonderful aromas. "Like "sugar plums dancing in your head," he thought smiled walking toward the bottom of the stairs.

The sounds of tiny feet jumped down off beds and pounded across wood floors. As always there stood

Walter, cup in hand, a grin ear to ear. Robert and Eileen laughter and smiles mixed with Walt's and Suzie's. Both children skipped every other stair; no sense in wasting energies getting to the bottom yes?

Presents wrapped just a few hours ago were splayed perfectly across the floor under the lit spruce tree. Suze always meticulously wrapped and arranged each gift so each child would know which was theirs.

Using age/gender appropriate paper and wrapping kept the gifts easily identifiable. Never was there any argument over which gifts were for who. Robert and Eileen would stand mesmerized at the pot of gold under the tree. Walt's old Lionel chugged around the lighted tree. Half-eaten cookies and a half glass of milk left for Santa on the plate was just consumed by Walt minutes ago. Both children wondered how such a pile of gifts found their way under the tree. It really didn't matter, both salivated at the possibilities. Never sure where or how to start they never needed encouragement.

Suzie always exclaimed her own delight in the magic of Santa. Walt loved the sparkle and magic in her eyes on such occasions. "Well go ahead and open them," Suzie would announce.

In a matter of a few seconds, they pounced on each pile and tore open dozens of packages. Absolute glee was in the air as boxes from under the tree were being torn open. In the middle of the room a new pile was being created; all the mangled torn wrapping was building a fortress in the center of the parlor. Wanting more coffee required careful stepping across toys, boxes, and wrappings; Walt picked through the obstacles and carried his and Suzie's cup to the kitchen for a warmer brew.

"Darling, please pull the cakes from the oven will you?" she called out.

"Consider it done!" His voice was muffled. He feared he would be discovered stuffing one of the freshly baked cakes into his mouth.

"No tasting them until they are cool," he heard her giggle. Making his way again through the maze of boxes and toys he handed her the fresh cup of coffee.

"How are the cakes love?" she asked with a sly smile.

"What cakes?" his face reddened.

"The ones with all the crumbs on your face Darling!" she laughed aloud. "Guilty," he thought.

No matter how many gifts under the tree, the time to open each and discover the prize always seemed too short. Eventually, a choice was made to play with one gift, try on some clothes or ask if they could go outside to try out the new toy.

For just a few moments every Christmas morning Walter and Suzie had time alone; soon clothes would be changed, church attended and the day's preparations would begin. Christmas day was a day to indulge in every delight indigenous to families. Regardless of ethnicity tradition or customs, Christmas was the day of sharing; remembering times past, people who have passed or simply indulging in the delicacies reserved only for such a day.

But for now, Walt tapped his lap inviting Suzie to sit. She snuggled in his arms so together they could stare at the lights shining on the tree. The angel atop shone especially brightly that year; enough to make Suzie take notice, "Look Darling. Look how much more bright the angel atop the tree shines this year." It was true. It did seem much brighter that year. Walt was never so happy, never so content and never so very much in love.

Suzie inhaled deeply and let go of a deep sigh. Her face nuzzled his neck. The kids were busy with all their new gifts and the morning was still early.

Standing she took his hand and smiled slyly, "come on we have time before they notice we are gone." Like two schoolchildren they stole away to their bedroom. Before he had his pajamas off he was ready; so was Suzie. He laid his full weight atop her and easily entered her. Her hips rose meeting each thrust.

When you love someone there is no pressure. He kept up his momentum feeling her tighten and grip his entire length. He whispered to her, "that's it, baby, love me. Feel me, lover, and with that, she tensed every muscle in an exquisite orgasm.

Her tightening pulled him in deeper. No longer able to hold back he exploded deeply. Each thrust spilled his love deeper inside. Finally, all that was left was his exhaustion laying on top of her listening to her heavy breathing.

Eventually, he raised his head and kissed her face, her cheeks and then kissed her with a passion and love only two people sharing such emotions could ever know.

~#~

In the kitchen, she stood at the sink and their son asked, "Are you alright mom?" She blushed again. Her red hair was a tangled mess, her skin still tingled and she was sure she smelled of sex.

"Yes, I'm fine love. Did you like all of your gifts?" she asked to change the focus away from her.

"Of course he did!" Walt announced walking into the kitchen. "With all those presents who could be disappointed?" He grabbed her from behind to nuzzle the back of her neck. "I love you Suze!"

"I love you to Darling." Suzie was happy.

~#~

Walter woke himself with his own snoring. He sat up straight and stared around the room. He was in those few moments of waking in a strange place where in time he would recognize where he was. The radio had been turned off and he had been covered in a blanket. The tree was still lit and new sounds filled the space. The day shift was on duty. New faces, new tasks to be completed, Walt stood and stretched. Hot coffee, hot breakfast would be available in the dining area. He decided to peek in on Suzie along his way. He opened the door slightly. She was sound asleep; staff had already changed her clothes and linens. Perhaps even gave her a sponge bath. Either way he decided food and coffee were needed now.

The dining area was genial at best. The aromas of food were always mixed with the odor of astringents and soiled adult diapers. The serving table was plentiful, filling his tray with plates of eggs and sausage, some potatoes and toast. Setting the tray down, he poured a cup of coffee into a huge ceramic mug and drizzled in some coffee cream. A quick stir, a reach for a powdered donut, he lifted his tray and searched for an empty table. He was grateful the rest of the staff and residents left him alone that morning.

Never one to be religious, Suzie taught him to be grateful. A short prayer of "grace" complete, the knife and fork dug into the plates and began to satisfy his hunger. For a few minutes that morning he forgot about Suzie's illness. He was grateful for the food, but feeling greedy; focused on his own hunger, he stood to replenish his plate with more eggs and this time, bacon. Spooning food deep into his mouth, Walt realized he was ravenous. He paused only a brief moment when the "code" alarm lights flash. He was used to such codes. The facility was a place where people went to die and such events more often pass unnoticed by everyone except the family of the deceased.

Walter glanced up with his coffee cup and saw the Code Team run past. They were heading to the other wing past the media room. Few stragglers from staff followed. Everybody has morbid curiosity he thought. All excitement passed; Walt turned his attention back to his breakfast. He couldn't seem to eat enough.

"I need to cook more for myself," he mumbled shoving more food. This time a parade of EMT's and Code staff reversed their way and headed to the emergency entrance. Oxygen masks and the usual mountain of emergency equipment surrounded the gurney and attending staff hid the patient's identity. As the stretcher passed it wasn't obvious who it was, but he thought it was a man.

~#~

Walt packed in more of his breakfast. Strangely he did not remember ever being this ravenous. The alarms sang a second time. Within moments the staff was alerted and at full attention. Barely able to pull his attention away from his plate, he never noticed the parade of staff and EMT's moving in the halls.

Oblivious to all the emergency activity, he carried his plate back to the kitchen drop off; thanked the server for the delicious meal. She acted as if he wasn't there, "Odd, she ignored me," he thought.

~#~

The hallway near Suzie's room was a din of noise. Doctors barked orders. Nurses and staff ran to the media room carrying IV's and pushing carts. Lights along the corridor flashed their usual warnings. "Wish they would shut those off," he thought.

~#~

A person experiencing partial deafness understands how surreal life moves with the loss of one of their senses. Even though one sense is lost, the remainders are keen and astute. You still "see" you still smell, feel and taste. Just there remains this pervasive quiet, like swimming under water, you are aware of sounds but cannot distinguish that which is going on around you.

Walt's ears "rang". He could hear, but more like playing "tin can phone," the game his kids played by stretching two tin cans across twenty feet of string; never sure if you were truly hearing the person speaking or if you heard because they were still so close.

"Damn! What's the matter with me?" he wondered. Sounds were there and then gone. He seemed to lose any sense of smell or taste. Lights flashed continuously around him. He neared Suzie's room, passing her neighbor's room. He turned and noticed the neighbor's door remained open and she was sound asleep. Oblivious to life while deep in her narcotic slumber. Nurses and staff exited Suzie's room. Walt stopped just outside and wondered why they were there.

~#~

A thousand times he entered her room; a thousand times he would see her asleep with sounds of electronic medical equipment saving her life. This time, he saw her bed empty, all equipment silent and dead.

Standing alone Walt tried to take it all in, "What's going on?" he asked himself, "Where is my Suze?"

Environmental staff pushed open the door. Walt turned; as if they walked through him, their attention was directly upon stripping and cleaning Suzie's bed.

He stood and stared at their work. Direct, competent and antiseptic. Linens stripped, the rubber mattress was being sanitized. Standing in total confusion, satiated from breakfast, Walt wondered if he was in the right room. In his muffled state of hearing, he wasn't sure what he was hearing, but it sounded like Tommy Dorsey, Guy Lombardo, and Bennie Goodman music.

~#~

"Hi Honey," Suzie called out. Walt's eyes moved from the hospital bed to the sound calling his name from behind.

Her smile never failed to warm him; always managed to radiate her love of life, her children, of him and of herself.

"Hello Baby," he heard himself say; they communicated in silence.

Walt turned his attention to a scene which melted his heart. Those old familiar feelings of love and admiration welled inside his soul. He relished his love for her, recalling once again a youthful love they so often shared. Suzie was standing there; her familiar red dress shrouded her in a mystical aura. Silken hair flowed as if in a gentle breeze, like the day they stood at the shore. At first, he was disoriented. Suzie was once again vibrant, younger and so full of life. Billowy wavy red hair with no gray; her signature giggle, broad smile and emerald eyes staring at him, he heard her words, however, she never spoke.

Walt extended his arm out revealing a khaki length of cloth adorned with military patches and polished brass buttons all in a row along the cuff line. Stunned to see he was wearing his old military uniform. Wanting to confirm what he was seeing, he glanced over at the mirror in the room; it was completely blank. However here they were, together in her room.

Past aches and pains had left his body. Nerve damage and arthritis no longer apparent, he took her by the hand. It was warm and tender just like the first time they danced. He held it up and out; his right hand cupped the small of her back.

The woman he danced with over sixty years ago was the same woman he danced with today. Nothing changed; she was the same Suze from the Grande. He was grateful he never let her go. She took him by the hand resting her left hand on his strong right shoulder, "stepping" into their dance. Wisps of hair tickled his nose. Chanel No. 5 seduced his senses.

Always exquisite. Always endearing. Always demanding perfection, they floated across the well-oiled floor of the ballroom. Walt sensed even his singing would now be perfection.

Anticipating his thoughts Suzie smiled and made a request, "Sing to me Private." Walt pulled her in tighter. Everything about them was once again real. An orchestra softly began to play; Walt was in full swing as he spun her around the floor. He fought the urge to hum;

instead, he broke out into an unusual well-pitched voice and sang to his Suzie,

> Sunday, Monday or Tuesday
> Wednesday, Thursday or Friday
> I want you near
> Every day in the year...

Three Days of Darkness

By Jerry Pociask

"Throughout history, it has been the inaction of those who could have acted; the indifference of those who should have known better; the silence of the voice of justice when it mattered most; that has made it possible for evil to triumph."

Haile Selassie

Copyright © 2017 by Jerry Pociask

This book is a work of fiction. Names, characters, places, and incidents are either products of the author's imagination or used fictitiously. Any resemblance to actual events, locals, or persons, living or dead, is wholly coincidental.

No part of this publication can be reproduced or transmitted in any form or by any means, electronic or mechanical, recording, by information storage and retrieval or photocopied, without permission in writing.

Prologue

One can never prepare for what may happen when they are cold, alone and in total darkness. Complete isolation is identical to a prison's solitary confinement. Powerless in the dark, dissimilar sounds play games with previous certainties of the mind. You hold your hand in front of your face, betting it's actually getting light outside, then slump further into depression when you admit to yourself it's not. Cold can be insidious. It takes you very slowly. At first it owns your extremities. Fingers and toes turn hard and white, frozen into stumps with no blood flowing to warm them. Attempts are made to curl toes inside boots, checking for some sensation, and then hoping for that endured pain when they slowly thaw. Somewhere along the way our body starts an accepted natural physical reaction for warmth by shivering. Few exceptional outdoorsmen understand. Shivering is the precursor to death. If nothing is done from that point on, soon the body will slip into a trancelike sleep, never again to wake.

~1957~

Gerry loved his dad; his dad was his hero. Gerry also loved his mom. She always made sure her family was well taken care of, but, his dad? He played catch; took Gerry fishing. Not all that big of a deal except his dad hated fishing. His dad's sport was bowling, but Gerry loved fishing. Gerry adored just being with him. The smell of his old stale R.G. Dun was always positioned in the crook of his mouth ensconced in an ivory cigar holder and became a part of his personality.

Gerry's dad had a hard life as a kid. Sent off to an orphanage at age three after his mom passed away giving birth to a younger brother. There, he spent eight years constantly hungry. The orphanage was a second thought for the Church. In fact, he mentioned they received great box lunches after a KKK march in the local city. Later he would only remember the food and not the political affiliations. To a young child, they didn't care about politics when they were hungry. Gerry suspected his dad was determined to share his life with his own children in a way he never was afforded. Thus the family never went hungry. Gerry's dad took care to insure they participated in all the events available he could afford, in time and dollars. Perhaps this reasoning led him to "teach" Gerry a lesson one evening in July when Gerry was four.

Gerry's dad loved beer; he was never without a cache in the basement refrigerator. Gerry became his father's shadow. Wherever his father was, Gerry was there. Going to the store wasn't about candy or sweet drinks, it was a chance to be with him. He would never hesitate to point out something of interest as they walked through a store. Gerry thought his dad was an encyclopedia filled with bottomless bits of information. Life was good. Gerry was happily secure until one humid July night became a night Gerry never understood and never forgot.

Gerry's dad was getting ready to make a "beer run". By instinct Gerry stood by the side door anticipating a usual trip to the store with his dad. "Can I go witchyou" Gerry asked? Any other time his dad would smile; inviting Gerry to join him on the front seat of the emerald green '55 Chevy. This time his dad stopped, turned to face Gerry and said, "It is time you learn to speak clearly son, it is NOT "witchyou", it is WITH YOU!" He emphasized those two words pointing his stump of a finger at Gerry's chest. Maybe it was the cigar holder that caused Gerry to not hear what his dad was saying. Instead Gerry repeated his usual, "witchyou."

"No! With you," his father repeated. Gerry's face started to redden and burn feeling an anxious moment. In Gerry's growing angst he again plead, "Can I go witchyou dad?" This time, almost in anger Gerry had never experienced his dad replied, "You cannot go with me until you say, "with you." "Say it," his dad demanded. Gerry could feel his face getting warmer. He started to cry. All Gerry could blurt out in desperation was witchyou". Once again his father corrected him, "With you". Say it or stay home. Tears flowed harder; all

Gerry could manage between his tears and a runny nose was a feeble "witchyou". Arms loaded with an empty case of returnable beer bottles, his dad turned and walked out.

Gerry ran outside crying and begging, "Please let me go witchyou." Watching his dad climb into the old Chevy and drive away, Gerry was left standing by the curb, watching the red taillights disappear around the corner. Gerry was devastated. His dad never left him behind. Gerry felt abandoned.

Eventually, Gerry's tears stopped and he took himself back inside to his bedroom. Later he heard his dad come home and chat with his mom. With muffled voices Gerry heard his name mentioned and he assumed they were talking about him. Gerry pretended not to listen. That evening, everything was either forgotten or ignored and all was back to normal. At the age of four, who would have thought Gerry would be scarred by his inability to say "with you" and being involuntary left behind?

Gerry never felt as alone as he did that day well except for that time in later years when he played high school football. Gerry was "special teams, i.e. kickoff team. That meant he only played when his school would win the opening kick-off toss or they scored. When they did score he got to play on the extra point team plus the kick-off after the score. The day his parents decided to come watch a game, his school lost the toss and never scored once the whole game. Gerry never played a second of field time. His parents sat along the sidelines on a chilly autumn day, waiting for their son to play, he didn't. Later that afternoon, embarrassed and still licking his wounds, Gerry opened the fridge searching for his bottle of Coke. Seeing it was gone he asked, "Did someone drink my Coke?" His sister yelled from the living room, "I did!" Upset Gerry retorted, "Why the hell would you do that? I was saving it for after the game." Without missing a beat his dad gripped that same ivory cigar holder between his teeth and hissed, "You never even played. Why do you think you deserve it? I told her she could drink it." Crushed and defeated, Gerry again retreated to his room to read, listen to music or quietly lick his wounds, usually all three.

It wasn't until years later when Gerry was ordered by the Church to see a psychiatrist about his drinking problem did he share the "witchyou" and Coke incidents. The shrink used the opportunity to triumphantly diagnose Gerry's drinking problem. The shrink told him he needed to face at least these two incidents and man up; quit sedating with alcohol and move on with living. Gerry took a month long hiatus from saying mass until he thought he was ready. After the month he stood at the altar pouring a little extra wine into his chalice, adding only a drip of water as a "chaser". "It's good to be back he thought."

~1962~

St. Suzanne's was one of those churches the Archdiocese of Detroit spent hours knotted in decisions on how to finance the growth of Wayne County suburbs. Technically they existed in the confines of "Western Wayne," however they were the "fringe of growth" that lead to the newer suburbs, aptly named Livonia, Plymouth, Westland and Garden City.

Northwestern county snobs decided to rename Westland as "wasteland," Garden City as "garbage city, and Inkster, "stinkster." Often times aptly named.

Communities like Plymouth and Northville established their own roots, too far away for a simple "Detroiter" to worry about and utilize to add further growth.

St. Suzanne's school and parish was a block away from where Gerry lived. An elementary school, play grounds and a church became the neighborhood island of activity. The first church housed the school until a newer, larger church was built to accommodate the growing Catholic populace, making the old church into a gym and auditorium complete with a stage. Across the street was the rectory and convent. Behind the church and school, expansive playgrounds, parking spaces and baseball diamonds provided hours of neighborhood gathering places. The basement of the school functioned as a dance hall, cafeteria, and nuclear fall-out shelter.

Storage tunnels were packed with barrels of water and dehydrated food just in case Russia decided to make good on their threats.

Through much of the sixties life was good. Dads worked. Moms scrutinized the household activities by controlling budgets and their families. Neighbors met over fence rows, street corners or front porches for laughs, beers and gossip. Televisions were huge boxes filled with electronic tubes that took minutes to warm up enough to display a black and white picture tube. Programming wasn't always available. When nothing was being broadcast, "test patterns" were displayed until the next telecast. Nightly news was aired more than most kinds of programming. Every night ended with the musical sounds of the "Star Spangled Banner," grainy movies effectively timed to the music had military jets flying over groups of American flags and the White House. When the last note played it was immediately followed by static and the familiar sight of the same test pattern.

~#~

Life was almost idyllic. The days were regimented. Families shared meals--no need for television during meals. There probably was nothing on. Computers were yet to be produced commercially. Cell phones and texting were on creative drawing boards. Mondays through Saturdays were passed with little or no change one day from the next. But Sunday had its own validation. Most stores were not open for business. Sunday was a day of rest. Regardless of religious affiliations, most dressed in their Sunday go-to-meetin' clothes. The parishioners at St. Suzanne's were no different.

~#~

Parades of families filed inside filling hard oak pews. As I mentioned, back then people dressed "up" for church. Women the age of sixteen or more always wore something on their heads, even if it had to be a piece of tissue bobby pinned to their hair. The men? Many men owned one tie and one suit. Every Sunday it would be pulled out of a closet strewn with moth balls, dusted off and worn. Shirts were heavily starched and ties were ironed. Saturday afternoon's KIWI shoe polish turned dusty cracked leather shoes buffed with a horsehair brush, back into the mirror image of their original selves.

Kids were dressed in some sort of clothes that did not resemble sandlot attire. The organist played somber tunes from the stacked pipe organ in the loft. One time in the '70s, Gerry became friends with the kid playing the organ. During communion Gerry recognized a very slow rendition of "Stairway to Heaven" by Led Zeppelin.

When the church was satisfactorily filled, the organist would stop playing. The crowd settled in and prepared. Few coughs or whimpers from newborns were quickly silenced and latecomers grabbed the closest available pew. Sometimes the ushers would push people along in the pews to make room for late arrivals.

Always a priest and the two altar boys entered the apse from the sacristy. To be sure everyone's attention was had, the first altar boy rang the bells. The second carried a three ton mass bible for the day's liturgy; the priest, his own chalice and paten covered in a linen cloth. Three brass bells were hung on the wall with a pivot attached to a gold braided cord. Pull the cord and the bells would sing! This day was Gerry's turn to be the "ringer."

The congregation rose. The priest climbed red-carpeted stairs to stand behind the marble altar. Gerry and the other altar boy, hands clasped across each chest in the "prayer" position, dutifully took their places in front of the altar, where they bowed then knelt. Looking out over the congregation, the priest blessed the people and the mass began.

"Fratres agnoscámuspeccátano-strar, ut apti simus ad sacra mystériac elebránda." Father Gannon raised his hands once again welcoming his sheep.

~#~

Latin masses were rarely understood, however they were accepted as the pomp and circumstances of the holiest of holies. Perhaps the Latin held a mystical attraction to what few would ever truly come to understand.

Father Gannon was imploring them to follow along with words few understood, however his tone alluded to some kind of consecration of sainthood, a forgiveness of thinking about wanting the neighbors wife or some shit like that. Father Gannon went on, "Confíteor Deo omnipoténti, I confess to almighty God and, etvobis,fratres,/quiapeccá, to you, my brothers and sisters, "vi nimis cogitatióne, verbo, "that I have greatly sinned in my, ópereetomissióne, thoughts and in my words, in what I have done, in what I say and in what I have failed to do. Strimea culpa, mea culpa, mea culpa mea maxima culpa. "Through my fault, through my fault, through my most grievous fault."

This particular Sunday a raucous laughter echoed inside the high arches. Even the swirling fans that spun to cool the congregation did not deafen the laughter.

Gerry knelt in front of the altar, a chubby cherubic stance with hands clasped in front of his chest.

He cocked his head not daring to break the holy mass protocol and searched for any sounds of disturbance.

Father Gannon under no circumstances stopped his service. The congregation didn't react. Gerry felt a very cold clammy breeze as the laughter continued.

Gerry hauled himself back "to" as the priest appearing nonplussed continued, "Misereátur nostri omnípotens, May almighty God have mercy on us, Deus et, dimíssis peccátis no- forgive us our sins, and stris, perdúcat nos ad vitam, bring us to everlasting life. Ætérnam. AMEN"

Bent over kneeling on hard steps in front of the altar, pretending to be in a state of solemnity; a black cassock carefully pulled up over his feet so he wouldn't trip or fall, Gerry mumbled his part of the Latin responses. The white nylon alb draped his shoulders and fell across his forearms as he pressed his right hand against his chest saying, "mea culpa, mea culpa, mea maxima culpa."

~#~

Gerry felt an affinity to these words. Even back in sixty-two he had an inordinate feeling he was ordained to help and save others. He knew he wasn't worthy of much else.

A fat cherubic kid, with few friends and smart as hell, he later figured out that was why many didn't like him. Girls didn't like fat cherubic altar boys either.

He loved playing baseball and touch football until the streetlights turned on and parents called everyone home. Yet, he wasn't one of the popular kids.

Sister Theresa encouraged him to dance. He was quite good. He could throw a football; he could pitch a strike. He just never "fit" in. Nothing ever changed.

Gerry fell in love in the seventh grade with Nancy. A gorgeous blond-haired, green-eyed, Polish girl who made his pecker hard and his face blush.

He never had a date with her per se. He had asked her out. She said she would meet him for an autumn hayride. She did.

They sat and talked on the forty-sum mile bus ride out of the city to some farmer's fields. There was a distinct aroma of autumn, fires and horse manure. The whole time around the fields and woods they sat next to each other on a dray filled of hay. It was a lovely night even for Gerry. He was inexperienced and immature yet he joined right in as everyone threw stalks of rotting hay at each other. They were laughing when anyone who managed to get an unsuspecting handful of hay down their backs.

For Gerry, it was one of his best nights. The ride home on the darkened bus found him wanting to kiss her. She was exquisite and he was a coward. He never did kiss her. Never spoke to her again either. Years later, he found out her step dad molested her and she left the earth. It wasn't his being fat or ugly or anything. He was a representative of the sex which repulsed her.

Mea culpa, mea culpa, mea maxima culpa.

~#~

"Misereátur nostri omnípotens
May almighty God have mercy on us.
Deus et, dimíssis peccátis no-
Forgive us our sins, stris, perdúcat nos ad vitam,
and bring us to everlasting life…
Ætérnam.

The congregation sat silently. New parents rocked and soothed their baby's need to scream out loud in defiance. In a panic, some parents walked out of the church to bounce or play with the now cooing child. Some mothers went to the bathrooms to breastfeed while others just went to the filled crying room to offer up a bottle of milk.

Sunday mass was a ritual. A "chit" or a notch earned just for showing up, a way to get into God's good graces. What's an hour of suffering when it gets you a few less days in purgatory? Mattered not the disturbance, the pain was offered up and ignored knowing the days in purgatory were surely being reduced.

Up at the altar, a solemn Gerry heard the laughter again.

~#~

Over time Gerry searched to fill a void. No matter how hard he tried to it in, it was never enough. The emptiness grew gradually. The sort of gradually where on a daily basis there was no notice of change. A year later the changes would put even the strongest into a tailspin panic. He tried filling the hours and the days by working at UPS. Then he cleaned restaurants. Nothing fit. He even forgot about Nancy. She was now a fading wet dream never to be seen again.

He enjoyed a few beers at places he hated. Many more he learned to hate. Always the same shit. Bartenders love the usual patrons. They know what they order, slide a number of freebies across the porcelain; patrons leave an extra buck or two tip and everyone is happy. Except the owner of course who gets fucked.

Over fifty years uncommon events altered Gerry's life. Kennedy was assassinated, Viet Nam divided a country over freedom of choice and allegiance to a country now even more divided by gender battles for dominance. Never able to relate to social or cultural events, becoming a priest was a safe place for Gerry to be.

Now as the priest who "said" the mass, Gerry became the sole actor upon the stage of God. Altar boys were a rarity, English replaced Latin. He poured his own water and wine and washed his own hands. The pomp and circumstance was lost. Led Zeppelin never was played again. The pipe organ remained silent except for Christmas or Easter.

~1988~

The Chicago Lounge was one of those drinking shit-holes where one could be obscure. Safe. In other words? Nobody gave a fuck about you. It was a quiet little place that some might assume was located in the "Windy City." Nope. A tiny neighborhood bar where drunks had lines of credit past three years. The blonde in the corner seat owned that seat for the past 30 years and at one time was built like a brick shit house where every guy came in wanting her and dreaming she'd go home with them.

Problem was simple. Blondie had aspirations of a better life. She always thought her white knight would ride in and save her. So, every local guy with a job and a hard on was "taken" for a drink. She may have even patted his pecker through tight jeans for another beer. But she was there with a goal, a purpose to meet a man who could take her away from all this shit.

Of course many tried but none were chosen. So now she sat there on the same barstool, the blonde hair now a wig, smiling at every uninterested guy who entered. She lost perspective of time. Twenty years ago she was somebody inside that little dump. Big tits and a tight ass wrapped in an equally tight short skirt commanded attention.

In 1988? Anybody new to the place either didn't notice or ignored her smile. They'd walk in, she'd toss her blonde wig and try to lift sagging tits atop the bar in hopes they would notice. Respectable sitting on the bar counter, but when she sat back, her tits slammed her knees.

Oh every now and then some old fuck from the past got to "pet" those fuckers. But that was about it. A drink bought you a play on the sweater. A Fuck? Sorry she still saw herself as she was thirty years ago, and YOU my friends, with your bald head and belly over your belt?

NO chance!

Gerry loved this place. Nobody knew him. Nobody who went to the Chicago Lounge went to a church. Any church. Ray the owner knew Gerry was a priest, but didn't give a shit either. Cash money for a Pabst was all he cared about. Gerry had lots of cash.

Being a priest was like being in the service, or for that matter jail. Three squares, warm bed with housekeeping and laundry, all for passing out tiny white wafers to the believers.

A good gig if you can get it. Plus it left the monthly stipend for Gerry to spend as he pleased. Hell, even a penitent parishioner who confessed his own transgressions with another parishioner who also served on the all-male church council, thought Gerry needed a nicer car to drive.

When Gerry saw these two council members in the drive of the rectory willing to hand over the keys to a new Cadillac? He thought to himself, "Bless you my brothers. You are forgiven."

And now Gerry pulled in behind the alley parking of the Chicago Lounge, hoping to slide in the back way and dominate his usual seat.

One o'clock, bright and sunny had no effect on the place except for the few patrons who voiced their objections to the sunlight that made the place look alive. Gerry always left the door open just a bit longer, wanting to blind the rest just long enough for him to take his seat. He figured when their eyes adjusted to the dark, they wouldn't know who he was anyway. But why take chances?

Confessions were conducted an hour before mass. A quick glance at his old watch said he had about an hour before he had to be back.

Ray walked up. Gerry said nothing. Magically a chardonnay appeared on the bar; nothing particularly extraordinary at a franchised restaurant. The Chicago Lounge? A whole new concept. Nobody asked. Nobody said. Except the blonde bimbo in the corner with floppy tits.

Gerry had been in this dump a hundred times. He loved it. Same people same reactions. Same shit; different day. He loved watching the people in there. He would nurse his beer and mentally pontificate his own superiority. Ray the bartender stuck on slippery floorboards forced to smile and sell a buck-fifty beer.

There was that guy who worked at Ford who "punched" the clock every day at 7:38, drove to the "lounge", drank his breakfast and lunch, then showed back up to work at 3:38 to punch out. Lunchtime was a negotiated paid holiday by the unions so nobody ever wondered where he went. About an hour later he was back and Ray always had the same beer iced and ready on the bar waiting his return.

Gerry would sit there in "street clothes". A collar would raise too many questions, sipping his beers or cheap chardonnays wondering if any of these patrons ever asked for his forgiveness in a confessional. He never thought about it long. He just wondered is this all they had in life.

Then there was the blonde. Gerry wondered who she was. Even imagined he knew her, and then realized he was already too drunk to think back that far. Plus he was priest. Often times he made a note to say the Act of Contrition for thinking about screwing the blonde. It never worked. Sometimes he would lie in bed regretting his vow of celibacy and wondered just what it would be like with her in bed.

Every time the door opened the big-titted blonde had hope. Maybe that was why she kept coming back. Cigarettes, moldy beer smells and a steady flow of regulars always gave her hope, she always hoped that maybe he was the one. How many of these oil soaked greasy guys ordered a Chardonnay? Only Gerry. She always hoped and was always disappointed when he never looked her way. In solace she buried herself in a ceramic soup bowl filled with beer nuts, and motioned to Ray for another beer.

One particular Saturday afternoon, Gerry was having a lot of fun. Unfortunately, he had to head back to say confessions. Priests started taking turns to say mass and confessions. Some churches were closing and the diocese wanted to consolidate to reduce costs. This was one of those nights where Gerry had to go sit in some other church and hear confessions. Ray brought him a shot of rye. Not for confidence, just to help Gerry through almost two hours of, "Bless me father for I have sinned" bullshit. On the way over to the "sister" parish, Gerry decided a wee pint might help him through.

May 19, 1988

"Carlos Lehder Rivas, of Colombia's Medellin drug cartel, is convicted in Florida for smuggling more than 3 tons of cocaine into US."

Gerry had his radio on in his new car and was half listening to the announcer and half giving a shit. All he knew was, he was late.

Catholics are weird about traditions and semantics. If a church bulletin publicizes confessions starting at 4 PM. Parishioners start showing up at 3:30.

So when Gerry walked in at 4:20, the cold stares alleged he was less than competent to forgive the litany of sins that include lying, swearing and impure thoughts.

Gerry draped his stole around his neck with the rest of the uniform, walked, or maybe stumbled a bit out of the sacristy, did the "genuflect thing and marched his way to the tiny cubicle as best he could; with dignity.

~2017~

"Blessed are you, Lord God of all creation, for through your good we have received the bread we offer you. Fruit of the earth it will become for us the bread of life."

Gerry found himself back in church. Gone were the bells and half the congregations, but he was comfortable. Being a priest was what he loved doing. Serving daily mass helped him to feel better in two ways. His congregation trusted him. Two masses a day allowed him legitimately to drink a bottle of wine before noon. The bishop never asked about the wine orders. The bishop was a lush as well. Stuck in a dirty old neighborhood where few lived, where the faithful kept a vigil of hope, and the rest didn't give a shit, was a perfect place for Gerry. Being a priest anywhere in the Diocese gave a man three squares, a bed, a housekeeper and clean laundry. It doesn't get any better than that.

~#~

The day started uneventfully. Nobody noticed clouds coagulating to turn the day sky into deep onyx. Thunderclaps sent arrows of lightening into the cold earth. Normally not an issue in the middle of summer, but is an issue two weeks before Christmas!

Gerry was saying mass. He poured his own water and wine into the chalice, pondering how he could fill his cup with enough wine and be able to offer the communicants a sip, leaving him a long draw at the end of mass.

"By the mystery of this water and wine may we come to see in the divinity of Christ who humbled himself to share in our humanity."

It was an early mass. Gerry had not had breakfast. Few people showed up for mass. Didn't matter he thought. "Extra rations of wine." He could pour the bottle into his chalice and no one would notice. Then, sit in the sacristy for twenty minutes while the next load of congregants showed up for the nine o'clock morning mass. Life was good. Being a church assistant pastor did have its privileges. By the next mass Gerry was fucked up.

Nobody noticed his slight stumble while serving communion to the few at the communion rail, for which he was grateful. Back at the altar to finish up communion he poured an extra sip of the wine into his chalice, wiped it out and repaired the tent made from the covered instrument, and then he heard a familiar sound. It was that same sinister laugh from before. He wasn't sure if he had too much wine or if it was that same bone chilling laugh he heard in St. Suzanne's years ago or, if for that matter anyone else heard it.

"Oh well," he thought and half shrugged his shoulders. He kissed the altar, genuflected, picked up his chalice and smiled.

"The left over wine will taste respectable," he thought.

~Evelyn~

Watching the threatening clouds form above, Evelyn attempted a rational answer in her mind. Her cell chirping pulled her away from the steamed glass pane. She answered. It was difficult hearing over the static.

"Hello," Evelyn answered, trying to hear a response.

"Evelyn, Gerry," the voice on the other side sounded panicked.

"It's begun. Get the candles out and start taping the windows."

Gerry was no longer an assistant pastor. His drinking bought him a demotion; now just a priest at St. Michaels. He hid his own insecurities and faults with a wee bit of self-righteousness. Yet, the parishioners liked him. So did Evelyn. She reminded him of Nancy so he was immediately attracted to her. He wished perhaps another time, another place. He respected his vows. So he decided to be her protector. Maybe that was why he chose St. Michael's parish? He could be a priest and vicariously be a man in her life. Instead, he said mass. He drank his wine. He read a lot thinking life was good. He and Evelyn really never were very close until after Jordan, had her accident. It is never easy to lose a child, let alone via a tragic accident. But the time it happened, Evelyn started liking Gerry well enough that he became one of the few men she learned to trust.

~#~

"Gerry?" she began to ask just before they lost the signal. She tossed the cell onto the chair. She knew what to do. Even had set out some of the things Gerry instructed would be needed. She spent hours searching the internet for pure beeswax candles; had "dipped" vials of plastic containers into the holy water fonts inside St. Michaels, and did the Home Depot trip for duct tape and black plastic bags. She had no idea her planning could ever prepare her for what was about to happen.

~#~

Evelyn began reviewing the list of instructions outlined in Father Gerry's directions.

"What the hell I am doing? This is crazy!" she scolded herself. The black plastic sheets blocked any light from the outside. Duct tape held it against the panes. She already knew it would ruin the paint finish, but she had her instructions.

"The landlord is an asshole so why should I care," she thought, assuring herself, feverishly applying a second layer of duct tape. The darkness had already begun to make the small apartment cold. A slight mist trailed her exhaled breath. Old places like this never understood poorly placed thermostats in the hall were inefficient. Hallways were always drafty. They welcomed the cold, and the thermostat always registered temperatures below the rest of the house, making the heat run continuously warming everywhere except the hall. Like most women, she never minded that; except when she was given her portion of the gas bill. Walking toward the wall in the hallway, she lit the dial with the small flashlight. Tapping the thermostat she listened quietly. When the heat "kicked on" she could hear the tiny gas flame torch the elements, then turning on the blower fan bringing a welcomed relief.

"Shit." Her voice was the only one sound amongst the deafening silence inside. She tapped once again against the plastic thermostat, one last hope; that banging the appliance would fix the problem.

"Maybe if I could kick it…," she muttered. She raised her chilled fingers and attempted to warm them against the thickening fog of her breath.

On top of the thunder and growing winds, Evelyn was convinced she was hearing voices; dismissing her thoughts convinced it was just the wind. Besides, right now she was just cold and wanted to get warm.

"Layering clothes is always a good way to protect against the cold," she remembered her asshole husband talk about hunting. She turned in the hall into her ex's room. Holding the end of the small flashlight with her teeth, she yanked drawers open searching for the long johns the asshole had left a few years back. All the neatly folded hunting socks, long johns and thick woolen mittens depressed her. It reminded her of the arguments they had. He suffered from obsessive compulsive disorder. Every morning he was up early and rearranging the fridge and the pantry, aligning cartons and boxes according to size; regardless of the fact they needed to be thrown away. As long as everything was in perfect order then his life was in perfect order; no one else's, just his. After he left her she decided she needed some counseling. Through a few sessions she learned how often times we marry a personality much like one of our parents. There was no doubt, she had married her father.

Evelyn hissed through teeth filled with flashlight, "Asshole, I knew someday you'd be worth something!" Painfully the memories from the accident and her husband's subsequent leaving crept in. She knew he would never forgive her for that.

Gathering up a huge ball of hunting stuff, her arms full, she beat a path back to the living room. Dumping it in a heap on top or the coffee table was like gathering firewood before crawling into the tent for the night.

"It's gonna have to work," she thought to herself, still burying memories and the pain of her past life with her ex and her dad.

~#~

As a child in Detroit, Evelyn gave a shit less about religion. Not that she didn't give a "shit" it was more that she needed more proof than was being offered. "Because I say it's so," wasn't the excuse she wanted to hear. The nuns would send her to the office for her "knuckle crunching" whenever she questioned their beliefs; which was every day. She was terribly spiritual, but gave up on attending any sort of church on her fourteenth birthday. Every Sunday she insisted she was old enough to go to church by herself. Her parents always attended the ten o'clock service. Her choice was the eleven fifteen. Less than a block away was a small café called "The Clock." At exactly eleven she walked in, bought a paper and a cup of coffee. She loved doing crossword puzzles. So, for an hour and a half, she would sit and drink coffee, working crosswords while her parents thought she was at church. One Sunday she was almost seventeen her mom asked just *which* church she graced with her presence. Knowing she was caught she replied sweetly, "Our Lady of the Clock." Her parents never again asked her if she went to church. By that time she learned to deal with her dad and she tolerated her mother's indifference.

When Evelyn's dad died she knew there was a God. She had never felt such a relief in someone else's death. She asked God to forgive him for what he had done; thinking that made her feel better. Standing at his casket she stared at a lifeless body. The cold indifference of the funeral home allowed her to forgive. In her parochial school Evelyn would argue, "Forgiveness is never about the other person; rather it's always for our own benefit." She could never understand how saying "I forgive you" wasn't somehow terribly arrogant. Comments like that always earned her a trip to see Sister Coronata, the Principle for a knuckle rapping with a wooden ruler.

Never having bought into all that Catholic bullshit she still managed to have faith. There was someone more important than the rest she believed. She always felt it should be *that one* person who was more important and had the right to say "I forgive you" not us.

~#~

When she met Father Gerry she saw he was not like the others; he made her see and feel differently. He wasn't without his own faults, he would really piss her off when he would start his pontificating, and nonetheless she liked and respected his opinions. After he spoke to her about the coming "Three Days," she was skeptical, this shit scared her.

"Gerry was too fucking convincing," she thought and this shit scared her!

Her "faith of a mustard seed" wasn't. She always managed to plant even the tiniest morsel of doubt during times like these. So she decided she would listen to Gerry's advice.

"It can't hurt right?" she convinced herself.

She checked and rechecked the windows for the coverings. A quick glance at the bottles of water and dry goods on the counter assured he she had enough to last for at least four days; longer if she rationed herself.

All the while she heard Gerry talking to her, "Do NOT leave ANY window open to the outside and NEVER under any circumstance look outside or open the doors until AFTER the third day!" That was the constant warning that resonated inside her head.

Fingers rotated the beads on the old rosary Father Gerry had given her. "Blessed, by the Pope," he proudly exclaimed. Digging down deep her memory came back easily.

"Our Father Who art in Heaven hallowed…" She stopped suddenly, remembering she was supposed to pray the "Creed" holding the cross on the rosary. Shoulders shrugged; embarrassed she could never remember the words to the "Nicene Creed". Half way through the first decade of beads her eyes moved across toward the sheet of instructions lying next to her on the sofa. At mid-sentence frozen fingers and shaking hands managed to lift the thin paper to read the instructions.

"One more check won't hurt," she decided making one last check of everything listed:

- Lock all doors and windows
- Cover them with black plastic so no light can come in
- Sprinkle holy water on the jambs and thresholds
- Use sea salts to create a perimeter around the entire apartment
- Have enough food and water to last for at least three days
- Find all the warm clothes you can. There will be NO heat or power
- Light the beeswax candles at the first sign of darkness
- Put the dog outside with enough and water to last four days

<u>Under NO circumstance are you to open any door or window until AFTER the 3 days!</u>

Gerry underlined the last sentence in warning.

~#~

After Jordan's accident, Evelyn and Father Gerry started becoming friends. She even started going back to church. Most priests would have required someone like Evelyn to attend confession at first before receiving communion, not Gerry. He was of the minority; he wasn't bothered by anyone who decided to leave the church. Instead, grateful for their return; he welcomed them with open arms. After the accident, Evelyn needed someone to forgive her. No one did. They all blamed her for not "watching out" for Jordan's safety.

~#~

Jordan was only out front for a very few moments when Evelyn heard the screech of tires. Her intuition told her something was wrong and she became nauseous. By the time she ran down the steps and saw the crowds, she knew. Her screaming parted a few people until an older gentleman grabbed her to try and stop her from going further. She remembers her own screams and his begging her to not go on. Evelyn pulled loose and saw Jordan's broken body lying in the street. Finally, in a heap he led her away. For hours the man sat with her on the neighbors stoop. He never left her side. Emotionally and spiritually she was vacant.

A child should never die before a parent. Being a parent, one knew eventually the child would grow up and leave to start their own lives. It was difficult being alone. Knowing a child moved a thousand miles away starts a loneliness that can be easily cured by a card sent, a call made or a surprise visit.

However when a child dies, any hope of ever being a part of life events, never hearing a voice or seeing that smile again, creates an incurable emptiness.

Father Gerry presided over Jordan's funeral. Evelyn felt a sense of calm during the first mass she attended in years. Gerry's words for the homily touched everyone but her. She was there only in the physical.

The graveside services weren't much better. She knew her daughter was in the casket. What she couldn't comprehend was she would never touch or hold her daughter, ever again. The piercing glares from her ex, only added to her guilt.

Slowly the cemetery emptied of the living. Two were left. Evelyn stood staring at the small casket covered in flowers. Gerry stood behind as distant support. Eventually he came up and gently took her arm leading her back to her car. Offering to drive her back, she declined. He handed her his card and invited her call any time. Handing her his card comforted him into thinking he was being there for her in support.

~#~

Sitting on the sofa shivering, Evelyn managed to smile at herself, recalling the first time she went back to confession. The light wasn't on over the confessional so she walked right in and knelt. She could see Father Gerry through the blurred sound screen waiting patiently for her to start. Like many prayers she hadn't said in years, she forgot how to start saying her confession.

"I don't know where to start," Evelyn whispered through the plastic screen. She was relieved that the priest couldn't see her in the dark. In fact they always had the lights on the priests' side so he couldn't see who was on the other side.

"What would you like to say," Gerry's soothing voice asked?

"It's been so long since I did this, I am not sure where to start," she responded.

"Welcome home," Father Gerry chuckled. Through the screen she could see him offering her his blessing; she awkwardly made a sign of the cross with her right hand.

"At least I remembered to use my right hand," she thought.

"Let me help you," Gerry offered, "again welcome back. I am sure you feel obligated to say you had impure thoughts…" Evelyn laughed at that one. "…but God already knows your sins," he went on, "so why don't we make it really simple? He forgives you."

Years of emotions she held inside began to flow out, tears welled in her eyes. In relief Evelyn readily agreed.

"Thank you" was all she could muster. With a slight chuckle she asked, "Does that mean I will be here for hours on my knees praying forgiveness?" Now it was Gerry's turn to laugh. She liked to see he was more than a priest; human actually. Through the blurred plastic she saw a warm and hearty smile that made her trust this priest.

~#~

After that initial confession they developed a trusting friendship. Evelyn started to attend mass every now and then. Sometimes they had coffee after. On one particular Sunday she felt more like sharing.

"I used to skip mass on Sundays and hang out at a local café to work crosswords and drink coffee," Evelyn started the conversation.

"I never thought in a million years I'd ever go back. So why have you been so friendly with me Gerry," she asked?

Gerry stared at his coffee cup spinning the rim round and round in anticipation of her eventual question.

"Evelyn, I am not sure why, but I think we have met because I am supposed to teach you something. Do you believe in coincidences?" he asked.

Evelyn watched him nervously play with his coffee cup and was not sure she wanted to know why he asked her or what his answer was. She inhaled deeply recalling past experiences, "Why do you ask?"

After a lengthy pause Gerry started: "Evelyn, have you ever heard of the Three Days of Darkness?"

"No, should I" she asked relieved he wasn't looking for something else.

"Not many have." His focus stayed on the black coffee in the cup, "but I think it's time you and I had a serious talk."

For what seemed like hours; Gerry slowly outlined the prophecy of the Three Days of Darkness, the end times, the "come to Jesus" realization for perhaps eighty percent of the world. Evelyn couldn't help but see him becoming an evangelist so strong in his beliefs. When he finally finished, he pulled a few handwritten sheets from a yellow legal pad from his vest pocket. On it he had written a list of instructions. Evelyn could not stop staring at the last sentence Gerry had underlined. After that they sat there for a long drawn out silence.

Eventually she cleared her throat not sure how to respond;

"So what the fuck am I supposed to do?"

His instructions were specific. He pointed to each and every point he had written emphasizing her exact compliance to each rule.

~#~

Now in her cold dark living room, wearing hunting clothes that were 3 sizes too big, Evelyn's frozen fingers placed check marks after to each item as she read them. Leaning forward near the single beeswax candle, Gerry's writing was easier to see. She felt more comfort as the candles illumination haloed out into her living room. The floor had a circle of light in the darkness giving her an illusionary safety zone. From the sofa she could barely see the groceries on the counter or even the front door, but at least she was able to see the last of the instructions Gerry had written.

"Beeswax candles always burn hotter and brighter than an inexpensive colored candle," his instructions explained.

The colored ones always looked pretty all lined in rows on shelves at department stores, but for now rainbows of color wouldn't make a damned bit of difference. Tapered delicate flames can be worthless against the bitter cold. Gerry had given her a candle lit from the Easter candle which Catholics bless on the Saturday just before Easter Sunday. The candle is supposed to be the light of eternity.

"Keep this candle in a safe place Evelyn." Gerry warned when he gave it to her along with a bottle of Holy Water.

~#~

"Wish this fucking candle would heat up this place!" Evelyn scowled under her frozen breath. Grateful now she had listened to Gerry, she kept it on the table in plain sight, as she completed her checklist:

Doors and windows were covered with blankets. Check!

Holy water was sprinkled around the frames and sashes.

Check!

Sea salts encircled the perimeter of the modest apartment.

Check!

Making mental notes for herself seemed assuring that all would be well, especially the last one; the thought of creating a crystal barrier against unknown intruders gave her a true sense of safety.

The dog was put outside with enough food and water to last at least four days. But it was the last instruction that bothered her the most.

"Evelyn," Father Gerry warned, "Under NO circumstances are you to open a window or a door until after the three days have passed. Not for anyone! Evil has a purposeful way to deceive us and they will do anything to trick you into opening a door or window. <u>UNDER ANY CIRCUMSTANCE, DO NOT OPEN THEM!</u>" Gerry again underlined that last sentence.

Satisfied she had followed her instructions to the letter, Evelyn settled onto the sofa to pray and wait. The wind was getting much stronger and her old apartment whistled and creaked through the old masonry. The black plastic covering the windows billowed in and out with increased pressure.

Every new sound, the tapping on windows from windblown branches, the obvious sounds of buildings being ravaged by the cold storm caused Evelyn to pray louder, "Our Father Who art in heaven. Hallowed be THY name....."

~#~

"Momma?" Evelyn jerked her head upright; she heard a familiar voice from behind the door. She sat frozen in silence, not even wanting to breathe.

"Momma, it's me momma. It's Jordan." Evelyn sat in disbelief. Shaking from fear and the cold, Evelyn attempted a breath.

When a person breathes in the cold, cool clean air it typically passes through nostrils effortlessly. This was different. The distinct aroma of sulfur made breathing difficult, like sucking wind through a small cocktail straw; short hard gulps attempted to fill her lungs which were exhaling rapidly from fear. Vaporous fog condensed tiny droplets on the fibers of the plaid wool blanket pulled around her back and neck.

Evelyn was a tall woman. She sat, legs crumpled under her chin in the soft leather sofa. She pulled every piece of clothing and blankets available around her like chain mail. Her hair was wound and wrapped by an old orange knitted hunting cap. The pile of her ex's old hunting clothes gave her some security; but hearing that voice was like a kick to the solar plexus that removed any hope for security. Pure guilt splayed over her entire being. Nothing could have prepared her for this moment. She was totally unnerved and hated the feelings of losing control.

"DAMMIT GERRY!" she said angrily, "You never told me THIS could happen."

"Momma!" the little girl's voice was no longer pleading but becoming demanding. "Open the door Momma. I'm cold."

Evelyn tried to shut out the voice in her mind, "Our Father who art in heaven…"

"Don't pray Momma it's alright. I'm just really cold and I need help Momma. I hurt myself and there isn't anyone who will help me. Open the door momma, please."

Evelyn's gloved hands covered each ear, she prayed louder; terror began to slowly creep in deeper, "…hallowed be thy name, thy Kingdom come.…"

"It hurts so much, momma!" Evelyn could hear their dog Mickey barking loudly just outside the door.

"Mickey's here now and he wants to come in too." The voice appealed pleasantly.

Evelyn prayed harder, "…thy will be done on earth as it is in heaven. Give us this day our daily bread.…" Painful shrills emanated from Mickey from behind the door. Evelyn stood straight up tossing her blankets in a heap around her cold anesthetized feet. "…and forgive us our trespasses as we forgive those who trespass against us.…" Mickey started to whine like a scared puppy.

"What's the matter Mickey?" the little girl sounded sympathetic. "Do you want to go inside too? Momma, Mickey wants to come in. Can you just let him back in? Please?"

Kicking the blankets aside Evelyn stepped closer to the door.

"DO NOT OPEN ANY DOORS OR WINDOWS!" she heard Father Gerry's admonishments in her head.

"There now Mickey, momma's going to open the door and we'll both soon be inside and safe," Jordan's voice sounded consoling. Evelyn couldn't help herself. Her instincts to protect like a sow bear started to take hold. She stood directly in front of the door and swore she heard her little girl crying. A shaking hand reached out pushing aside the dead bolt on the door frame. One hand firmly grasped the door handle and slowly began turning. The other was manipulating the multiple locks.

"Open the door Momma, please! I am cold and Mickey is hurt!" the voice knew it was winning.

Evelyn was not even aware of now whispered prayers, "…and lead us not into temptation, now and forever, Amen."

"This is crazy Evelyn!" she yelled at herself. "Jordan was killed four years ago in that accident!"

Her memory of that day flashed in her mind in a blind fury! Evelyn had never forgiven herself. And all this time she argued with herself about it not being her fault.

It was the first time she had allowed Jordan to cross the street without watching her. She had just had a huge fight with her ex. He stormed out once again leaving her to her own guilt. Jordan wanted to visit her friend across the street. Evelyn knew others heard the fight; not wanting the neighborhood to think they were fighting again, she relented. She could hear Jordan bound down the stairs in excitement. Evelyn heard the usual slam of the outer door. At first her mind wouldn't allow the sounds that followed the doors slamming shut.

Tires wailed haltingly. Mickey came to attention running toward the door! Motherly instincts grabbed

Evelyn by the throat. She knew what had happened and wanted to vomit as she ran outside. The car was sideways. The man stood in horror one leg inside the car. People emptied from the brownstones into the street. Evelyn pushed her way through; there was Jordan crumpled on the searing asphalt.

She was faintly aware of the driver saying, "She ran from between the cars…Oh GOD, I never saw her."

Sirens in the distance were on their way. She remembered an elderly man tried to prevent her from reaching Jordan. He plead with her to not go into the street, but she refused to listen. Others tried to help; all Evelyn could do was hold Jordan for the last time. The EMT gently pried her arms from around Jordan's still body; the elderly man reappeared with a stolen blanket from the emergency truck. He wrapped Evelyn in it, carefully, slowly scooping her up. Evelyn was in shock. She looked back and saw the EMT close and lock the back door. The truck left slowly with no need for the lights and sirens. The emergency was over.

~#~

"Momma" Evelyn heard the locks disengage from the jamb as she reached to turn the door knob. "Hurry Momma I'm cold and Mickey's hungry." The voice knew her weak points.

"DO NOT OPEN ANY DOORS OR WINDOWS!" Father Gerry words echoed again and again inside her head. She was building up the courage to open the door. Her head was swimming from the sounds outside, Gerry's warnings, Jordan's pleading, and her heart over ruling her head.

"Don't listen to Father Gerry, Momma. It's really ok to open the door. I want to see you momma, I love you."

Evelyn could no longer resist being a mother. For the second time instincts overcame her ability to reason. She smiled wanting to see her daughter just one more time. The door catch released and she flung the door wide in anticipation.

It was the last thing she would ever do.

~#~

Gerry woke up stiff and sore from sleeping in an old chair parked in the sacristy. The priests used the chair while waiting for masses to begin. A great place for a casual sit; awful for three days of sleep.

He carried in groceries and some pillows, candles were already there. Holy water was plentiful, the wine well stocked. The housekeeper decided to go home to her family. No dogs no pets, the parishioners were all at home. He thought about heading over to Evelyn's but called her instead. They got cut off but Gerry felt good about her being alright. After one last round around the churches perimeter, he lit the annual Easter candle that stood by the altar, moved into the sacristy, pulled on some warmer clothes, lit a few more candles and stockpiled a couple of cases of wine. The first clap of thunder was accompanied by the dull "pop" made by a wine cork pulled by the screw. Gerry poured a generous amount into a crystal glass and settled into the padded uncomfortable chair, ready to ride out the storm mainly by himself and his wine.

As the storm grew stronger and more violent he swore he heard voices talking, and at one point actually thought he heard his name called. Shrugging his shoulders he tossed it off to finishing his second bottle and opening his third. That was how he spent his three days in darkness; alone, in the dark and drunk.

On the morning of the fourth day, he heard the faint sound of birds singing and his candles were almost gone. He opened the door to the altar. The Easter candle had burned down six months of Sundays. Light shone through a dozen stained glass windows, leaving an eerie sense of gloom. Heading back toward the sacristy he extinguished the big candle, blew out the ones in the sacristy, relieved himself in the small bathroom, and started walking out. His crystal glass sat atop the counter with about fifteen bottles of wine. The glass was a little more than half-full.

"What the heck," he thought and downed the entire contents with a couple gulps.

Feeling a sense of renewed courage, Gerry opened the entryway to the sacristy. The shine was brighter than he anticipated, or else his eyes were still clouded by cheap wine. He shielded his eyes until he had his sunglasses on and stepped off the stoop.

People were slowly emerging from homes. The dogs left out barked and wagged tails when they saw their owners. A few houses were quiet and dark. There were a few driverless vehicles that ran into fences or tree. As he passed one he noticed the key was in the ignition and on.

"Out of gas," he whispered to himself.

Satisfied his immediate area was secure; he wanted to check on Evelyn. As he approached her complex the destruction apparently became more intense. Becoming anxious, he stepped it up nearing Evelyn's apartment. Some of the residents were standing around the front entry. He asked if anyone had seen Evelyn. One guy shrugged his shoulders and muttered something about not seeing anybody after all the last three days brought.

Inside the entry hall, Gerry took the steps two at a time. Anxiety was gripping his soul and he needed to know. Entering the long hall, almost every door was open or ajar. His heart sank. In his horror and disbelief, Evelyn's door was open. Near tears he stood at the threshold where salt was once poured. Windows were taped shut and covered against any light. The candles he gave her were completely burned down. Mickey was on the sofa and perked his head up when Gerry walked into the living room.

"Where's Evelyn Mickey?" Gerry asked. The dog sat there waging his tail and whined a little, probably more from being hungry for a day or so. Gerry searched the entire apartment, confirming his own fears. Everything was as Evelyn had left it except one thing. Evelyn was gone.

Gerry fell to his knees in shock, horror and tears. His best friend, his only friend whom he had tried to protect didn't listen, and was gone.

"Why didn't I come here instead of staying inside the church?" he wailed out loud. The guilt set in quickly. He didn't want to venture outside, so he stayed behind with his stock of vino and he would be was safe inside the sacristy. If his wine was safe, he was safe. Never in a million years did he think Evelyn would open the door. Gerry threw himself on the floor and cried. Cried for Evelyn, cried for his loss and cried in his own guilt.

~#~

The three days took its toll on many families. Lost loved ones simply vanished; disappeared with no trace. There was no television yet but Gerry wondered what happened to all those passengers and crew caught in mid-air. Worse yet, where would all those silver birds have gone without some sort of pilot on board? Emergency services and those who could help, cleared away the debris.

Within six months the damage was gone. Memories of loved one's became just that, a memory. Gerry's Bishop tried to "beat" the warnings by trying to drive himself home to his parents. He never arrived home. They found his car stuck against another car that was probably parked. The pastor's car keys were found in the ignition, motor not running and the gas tank was empty. The remaining bishop's elected Gerry as transitory pastor. He willingly accepted just so he could keep himself busy. It would help to forgive and forget his own transgressions during those three days.

~#~

Early Monday morning mass now was rarely attended by more than ten people. Gerry didn't mind. He was back to drinking. While five of the ten were still asleep, the other five were there undoubtedly because they were homeless. Churches were a refuge for the lost, tired, poor and homeless; none of whom paid any attention to the services. Gerry easily managed a few extra gulps of wine and nobody noticed his sway or slurred words as he ended services. Nobody noticed either when he grabbed the cruet with the left over wine from the side altar table. Most would have thought it was to be refilled and they would have been partially correct. He did refill the crystal cruet, after drinking what was left. Taking a few sips from the bottle, then refilling the crystal glass, he walked back out into the apse to set it back on the side table. He crossed the front of the altar and from the corner of his eye he noticed one person still sitting in the now polished oak pew.

Genuflecting at the center and in front of the cross of the crucified Christ, a familiar sound echoed through the vacant church. Familiar but empty, Gerry searched his memory of why it was familiar. As he stood there, the memory punched him harder than a right cross to the jaw. Pivoting on one foot he looked at the one remaining person seated in that pew. The "same" pew as his memory was becoming clearer.

"Good morning Gerry," he heard with a cynical laugh. "Remember me?" the man asked with a smile.

Gerry felt nauseous and weak. Trying desperately to convince himself it was caused by almost a bottle of wine and no breakfast. Gerry's eyes closed trying to erase the memories. Too late. The sight, the sound of that laugh; the smell, oh my God the smell; It was all coming back to him from that morning he served as an altar boy at St. Suzanne's back in 1962.

~#~

"What's the matter fat ass, aren't you happy to see me?" The words echoed across the spacious church.

He was stunned; he couldn't answer. The old man in front of him was an illusionary homeless person. Disheveled, needed a bath, and stunk like hell. Being called fat ass again riled a storm inside of him. His reaction of fury was certainly a sin, he thought.

Over fifty years of swallowed emotions were rising in his throat. Gerry double timed down the aisle lifting his cassock to his knees. Out of breath he confronted the bum with rage filled eyes and venomous intent.

"Who the fuck are you?" Gerry screamed.

"Well fat ass, you should remember me from back in the sixties. I am the one who has followed your every move since you started school. I always knew you were the one I was to have," he said.

The church's atmosphere shifted and Gerry could sense danger.

"What do you mean I was the one?" Gerry spat through thin lips.

Clenching his fists he ordered, "And don't call me fat ass again!"

The pause was long and deafening. Finally the man stood up and moved directly in front of Gerry, magically producing a soda bottle, "Coke" the man probed a little deeper. They stood eye to eye. Neither moved nor spoke. An emotional face off for supremacy. Gerry sensed he was about to lose.

After one hard swallow Gerry lost, "What do you want?"

"You, of course! All along all I wanted was to be "witchyou," came the reply. Gerry's face heated and reddened like that day back in 1957. The man smiled. Gerry tried to ignore the surfacing words and feelings from his past.

"You see, I will give this to you," the immoral bum continued. "I first thought you were a weak fat ass. I quickly saw you were not weak, lonely perhaps, but not weak. So, then I realized I needed a new tactic. Something that would prey, get it? "Pray," on your feelings. You gave me the opening I needed to gain ten yards. Remember the hayride and that blue eyed blond Nancy?" Gerry stared hard, too terrified to shift his eyes.

"Yeah old Nancy was a cute little shit. Too bad her step dad fucked her up. By the way, she liked you. Unfortunately her damage was done. Years before she could even admit what happened. Blamed herself for being, "naturally provocative" as the step ass had accused her.

"Then I needed something else. I thought maybe drugs, booze…God knows you were already addicted to food. So I decided booze was quick and easy. And you, oh you my chubby little fuck. You bought it all. I'd sit back and watch you as I sat in the corner of the Chicago Lounge, having all the other slimy fucks buying me drinks and feeling me up. Damn I hated that. But I endured thinking maybe, eventually you'd come around." He continued, "But no you little shit. You were a coward with Nancy and a coward with me at the bar. I waited. I actually thought you would eventually have enough beer in you to make your move on me. Maybe buy me a drink grab some ass or god forbid, try to get laid. I will say this, you do have honor in your resolve."

Gerry swallowed hard, "That was all you?" he asked. The whole time, Nancy, the drinking, the old broad? All you?"

"Of course you dumb shit," the man went on, "A clumsy piece of shit like you had no chance at much. So I had no choice but to give you a helping hand. THAT is what made you my special prize."

Gerry's head started to hurt. The nausea and dizziness increased. Must be the odor of lit matches making him sick he thought. "Go on," he asked faintly.

"I stepped up my game," the bum continued. I'd show up at your masses to check up on your resilience, and then I had a great stroke of luck. Remember Evelyn?"

A familiar rosy burn on Gerry's face was obvious which appeared to make the man smile. "What about her?" Gerry asked, now more terrified than ever.

"I knew you would like her. Nice smile. Nice ass. I also knew she was as fucked up as you. By the way, nice graveside service for Jordan," was his icy comeback.

"After you and Evie made nicey nicey and I kept thinking I'm gonna win, especially when she decided she could trust you. But damn man! You were scared shitless of women since you popped outta yer momma's belly, that's for sure."

Gerry had this intense rumbling in his lower bowels and thought he was about to lose it entirely.

"Come on man, don't shit yourself," the man said sympathetically, "you know you liked her. You just never had the balls. So I did the next best thing. Wine is such a wonderful aphrodisiac isn't it?" You "wanted" her but remained a coward. "So you started making excuses for your behaviors."

You gave Evelyn the combination to her safety for "the event," but you misread her own weakness. I knew she still ached over Jordan. Her mama-bear instincts would show up and I would win. My only issue was you."

He continued his speech, "I had to figure out how to keep you away from Evelyn's place for three days, and you and the holy grape gave me my answer."

Gerry was shaking and tears started to well up.

"Yeah ole buddy, you were strong against everything but the grape," now he was laughing.

"You convinced yourself that Evelyn would follow your instructions to the letter, and that you could drink yourself stupid for three days inside the church. You were right in two ways. You are stupid, and Evelyn followed your instructions all the way. Until I did my best ventriloquist act to sound like Jordan. Outside the door I could have convinced Evelyn I was her ex trying to apologize. Damn that was fun!"

Gerry spewed vomit across the floor, and the bum stepped back a little, "Missed me I see," the man said laughing.

Gerry knew this resident evil was right. He did everything he had said. He did love Evelyn as he secretly loved the adolescent Nancy. However, wine replaced and sedated his guilt and emotions so many times, he never supposed what was real or what was an illusion. And yes, he stockpiled wine, food, more wine and candles in the sacristy knowing he would be safe. He even called Evelyn to check on her but the call was cut off.

The evil read his mind; laughing he added "Yep, it was me who ended that call as well. Pretty good huh?"

~#~

Guilt can be insidious. In Gerry's case he wanted a drink. The pressure inside made him feel like exploding. Cold sweat poured through wine-infused chambers no longer filled with oxygen. His heart pounded a piercing uneasiness along his left side. His ears rang, his eyes rolled back. More vomit dribbled from his mouth. The fall to the floor didn't hurt.

~#~

Gerry woke up to the lights, the sounds of an ICU. The rhythmic pulse of machines is what kept him alive. Staff buzzed in and out of his room. He looked around. Above his head he could see the heart monitors registering normal. He was going to be alright. He gratefully sighed and turned his head.

There was another patient who shared this room. He could hear the similar yet dissimilar pulsing sounds from their equipment. Somehow, Gerry found this reassuring.

After a day or so, his "neighbor" was moved and Gerry was once again alone in his room. Waking from an afternoon nap, he was alone. Groggy from all the meds and drugs, he stared in bewilderment at a familiar evil he believed to be just a part of this dream. The stench and the evil grin said otherwise.

Stepping into the overhead lights the homeless man smiled. With a wink, a raised thumb and a pointed forefinger, he feigned the motion of shooting a pistol saying,

"Once again you won. But I will be back!"

Gerry collected up a weak smile and replied, "I'll be ready." For the first time the homeless man's smile disappeared.

About the Author

lifemanagementllc@gmail.com

A lifetime dedication of helping others to find their "greatness within" has led Jerry to become a successful business man, teacher, life coach and father. His own measurement of success is directly related to his ability to helping others find their way in life.

Check out his other work:

Grandma, Me, and Tree
Call me Grandpa

Contact Jerry here:

https://www.facebook.com/jerry.pociask?ref=br_rs
https://twitter.com/jerry_pociask
www.jerrypociask.com

Made in the USA
Lexington, KY
20 February 2018